The Foxy Hens Meet a Romantic Adventurer

The Foxy Hen Series

The Foxy Hens Meet a Romantic Adventurer is the latest book in the Foxy Hen series.

Previous titles:
Two Foxy Holiday Hens and One Big Rooster
The Foxy Hens Go Bump in the Night
The Foxy Statehood Hens and Murder Most Fowl
Chik~Lit For Foxy Hens

Purchase all these books at bookstores or at the publisher's website:
http://www.awocbooks.com

The Foxy Hens Meet a Romantic Adventurer

Charles W. Sasser
Jackie King
Peggy Fielding

Deadly
Niche
Press

Denton Texas

These are works of fiction. Names, characters, places, and incidents are products of the authors' imagination or are used fictitiously and are not to be construed as real. Any resemblance to actual events, locales, organizations, or persons, living or dead, is entirely coincidental.

Deadly Niche Press
An imprint of AWOC.COM Publishing
P.O. Box 2819
Denton, TX 76202

No Longer Lost © 2010
by Charles W. Sasser – All Rights Reserved.

Warm Love on Cold Streets © 2010
by Jacqueline King - All Rights Reserved.

Weeding Out the Problem © 2010
by Peggy Fielding - All Rights Reserved.

No part of this publication may be reproduced, stored in a retrieval system, or transmitted in any form or by any means, electronic, mechanical, recording or otherwise, without written permission, except in the case of brief quotations embodied in critical articles and reviews.

Manufactured in the United States of America

ISBN: 978-0-937660-66-9

No Longer Lost
Charles W. Sasser

Charles "Chuck" Sasser is author of more than 60 published books and thousands of magazine articles. Visit Chuck's website, www.CharlesSasser.com

*Susan —
Live life well
"Chuck"
Charles Sasser*

Chapter One

Josh Logan realized at the end of the fourth day that he was hopelessly lost in the Canadian wilderness. He watched the red sun setting behind dark banks of clouds as he paddled his kayak to the narrowing dead end of the salt water channel where a stream rushed fresh water down from the mountains. He paddled into the shallows until the hull of the kayak crunched barnacles. Tiny purple starfish littering the beach after the receding tide popped like packing bubbles under his feet when he got out of the boat and pulled it ashore.

He took a deep, weary breath. A week ago he had set out for Alaska via the Inside Passage of British Columbia. At some point he had taken a wrong turn in the morning fog. Since then he had encountered not a single soul. Nothing in this wildest, most remote country he had ever experienced except the occasional whale, a few harbor seals, some sea otters who resembled old men floating on their backs in a Miami Beach pool and, once, a bear that prowled around his camp most of the night.

At this rate, he was unlikely to make it back for his wedding. Maybe *lost* wasn't such a bad thing.

He dragged the kayak up to the permanent driftwood line and tied it off on a long painter so the returning tide wouldn't swamp it. He was lean and athletic with dark eyes and curly black hair trimmed short. He wore khaki hiking shorts and a much-soiled t-shirt pulled over a diver's wetsuit, booties with thick rubber soles, and a U.S. Army field cap. He felt much more comfortable in such garb than he did in the Brooks Bros. Suits tailored for him back in Chicago. An up-and-coming young investment banker, he grabbed at every opportunity to go rock climbing, kayaking or backpacking. He might have been reared in the city, but he was born to the wilderness. Golfing was an old man's game, and a boring one at that, especially when played with Elizabeth's father.

Elizabeth's father had big plans for him. So did Elizabeth.

Boardrooms could be far more savage than a jungle in Tanzania or a swamp in the Matto Grosso. Than here, lost somewhere in a labyrinth of channels, reaches and bays where *nothing* was tailored except by God.

It was after ten p.m. and would be getting dark soon. Josh lugged his camping gear in waterproof bags to above the high tide mark, into the conifer rainforest so thick that fleeing pine squirrels had to duck and dodge. Using a hand ax, he cleared a place to erect his tent. He unrolled his sleeping bag inside. He would sleep just fine tonight. The moss was nearly a foot thick and as soft as a mattress.

Camp made, he took his empty canteens and a stout hiking stick and returned to the beach. He followed it the short distance around to the mouth of the fresh water creek. Fish flashed in the water like quicksilver. No doubt the spring salmon run would attract grizzlies and blacks. He felt vulnerable without a means of defense, but Canadian law was so complicated with red tape that he hadn't even bothered to try to bring a firearm. Besides, he hadn't expected to end up lost where "few men have gone before." He loved the old *Star Trek* series.

He hiked upstream to where the water would be fresh and untainted by salt from the rising tide, climbing over and around boulders, driftwood, fallen trees and pushing through old growth as thick as fur on a sled dog. The bank of clouds now blotted out the low sun and the air grew hazy with the approach of evening. Once he glimpsed something large and dark in the forest on the other side of the creek. The hair on the back of his neck crawled. In this country, man didn't necessarily occupy the top rung of the food chain.

He proceeded a bit further before he knelt at a freshet of fast water. He cupped a palm full and tasted it. Cold and delicious. As he began to fill his canteen, he glanced up and saw something metallic gray and out of place in a field of green at a bend in the creek where the water deepened and pooled above the rapids.

Curious, he worked his way past the fast water to the pool, where he came upon a motor skiff seemingly cast aslant by the last tide into a gnarl of tree roots. It had not been here long; no barnacles encrusted its hull and only a single strand of seaweed strangled the outboard engine. People in the wild North Country would never be so careless as to lose a boat, not when it was their only means of transportation and *could* mean the difference between life and death.

There was nothing in the little boat except an empty fuel can and a fish landing net. He was turning away, not wanting to be caught far from camp after dark, when he noticed the bullet hole below the starboard gunnels.

Jagged edges of metal on the inside marked it as an exterior entry. A smear of dried blood on the operator's seat made the situation even more curious. It was a bit unnerving, what with the isolation and that vast silence of the North that suddenly seemed to collapse around him. He felt as though he had been cast with a corpse into an empty cemetery.

He looked around, but found no other sign of the boat's owner. On his way back downstream toward camp and the beach, he caught another glimpse of black movement in the forest. Why hadn't he braced the Canadian red tape after all and brought a gun?

Chapter Two

Foot-deep moss mattress or not, each sigh of wind through trees, a falling pine cone, the rustle of some small creature through grass jolted Josh awake. He lay on his back in the dark tent. The boat, the bullet hole and the blood must have unsettled him more than he'd thought. When he left Chicago to go on "walkabout" before the wedding, Elizabeth had chided him about his attraction to what she called "the middle of nowhere." What were the chances of his coming across a scene of human violence in "the middle of nowhere?"

Was the victim somewhere nearby? Dead, or perhaps wounded and needing help? That produced further consideration about the perpetrator. Josh had crawled into his sleeping bag fully-clothed, having changed into jeans and a blue flannel shirt. He hung the wetsuit outside as a makeshift "scare-bear." Now, carrying his sheath knife, he emerged cautiously from his tent to stand alert and listening beneath a canopy of conifers that made darkness hard and deep and seemed to magnify every sound to a threat level.

Although he knew he had more to fear in the streets of Chicago than in the wilds—last year he had been mugged in a parking lot—he couldn't suppress the something cold that coiled and uncoiled inside his stomach. It was his imagination, he tried to reassure himself. There was nothing out there.

He returned to his sleeping bag. He remained awake and was still open-eyed when dawn softened the night. He crawled outside and looked around. Morning fog had closed in, restricting vision. He opened a trail packet of ham 'n eggs and ate standing up.

The prudent thing to do was break camp, stuff everything back into his kayak, and paddle the hell out of here. He was lost and already running short of food. Whatever had happened here was none of his business. Why ask for trouble that wasn't his?

"Understand this," his future father-in-law would have advised. "The world is like high finance, only on a slightly broader scale. It's a dog-eat-dog world in which the cunning survive. You have to think of ole Number One, Josh. Take care of you and yours. Let others do the same. That's the killer instinct behind the success of the Reynolds Investment Firm."

Josh realized Elizabeth Reynolds had her father's killer instinct. She went after what she wanted—and she generally got it.

Josh was sweating even though the morning was cool, almost chill. His lips were dry. He drained a half-canteen of water down his throat. He felt like a frightened kid walking through a graveyard at midnight. He had never considered himself timid, but this might be a little *too much* adventure.

Still, somebody might be hurt or even dying out there in the woods. He could never forgive himself if he ran away without at least making an effort to check things out.

He armed himself with his sheath knife and hiking staff, jerked low the brim of his old Army fatigue cap and made his way around the beach and up the creek to the still pool. The boat remained undisturbed where he had left it. The sun was up, but no rays penetrated and the air was gray and turgid. Tendrils of fog creeping silently out of the pool, reaching to clutch the trees, reaching for *him,* reminding him of Stephen King's *The Mist.*

Humidity had made the blood in the boat more viscous. The empty gas can puzzled him. It didn't compute that anyone would run out of gas in this country; old hands always carried extra fuel.

Tapping the ground with his staff, he searched for footprints or other sign that might provide a clue as to what happened. Circling further from the pool, he came across a game trail and followed it upstream until it branched off, one feeder shooting uphill through thick rainforest, the other continuing along the creek.

He had an uneasy feeling that he was being watched. He thought he heard something moving in the underbrush.

"Who's there?" he challenged.

No response. The fog was thicker here, as though a cloud had descended on the mountain. Like the moors in *Wuthering Heights.* He drew a deep breath and followed the uphill trail, keeping a sharp watch, weapons clutched in white-knuckled fists. Jamie Lee Curtis was always going down into dark basements where you knew Michael was waiting ready to pounce on her with razors clacking. In real life, people didn't do things like that. They got the hell out of Dodge.

Josh stopped and looked back. He looked uphill.

"Is there anybody out there?" he shouted. "I'm here to help you."

That made him feel foolish—talking to a bear most likely. Or to a dead person.

Okay, okay, he had made the effort. Time to forget the whole thing.

He started back toward the creek and the trail junction. He heard movement again, behind him, and wheeled around just as something dark and erect on two feet darted through the swirling mist. It was only a glimpse, but it chilled the saliva in his mouth. Moments later came an eerie scream, not fully animal but not human either.

What the hell was that?

It took every ounce of his willpower to hold his ground and not bolt headlong for camp.

Logic and reason warned him not to go down into that dark basement. Along with the fear, however, came a healthy dose of the same curiosity and sense of adventure that propelled him into wild and remote realms in the first place. Although he watched old monster movies with Elizabeth, that didn't mean he *believed* in monsters.

Whatever flashed across the trail would have left footprints. He promised himself that he would go and take one quick look, then hightail it out of this weird dark forest of fog and sounds.

Sweeping his staff back and forth, as though to clear the way of fog or whatever lurked in the fog, he made his way to where he spotted the dark shape leap out onto the trail. In the soft loam at his feet appeared a barefooted track that looked almost human, with five toes and everything—except it was easily eighteen inches long and eight inches wide. The bare footprints of a giant.

Josh hadn't believed in *Jack and the Beanstalk* since he was four years old.

Chapter Three

Elizabeth was a monster freak. She had rather stay home on Saturday nights to watch SyFy Channel than go out. It was "the most dangerous night on TV." With Komodo lizards the size of houses and giant cobras gobbling up tourists who weren't smart enough to stay out of the basement. With underground worms that outran Ford pickup trucks and mutant crocodiles that leaped out of the water to snatch sexy water-skiers.

Sometimes, he persuaded her to run to bed for a quickie between *Tremors* and *Creature from the Black Lagoon.*

One night they watched *The Legend of Boggy Creek*, the supposed true story of people around Fouke, Arkansas, terrorized by a creature that left footprints like the one in the trail at Josh's feet. But what else could you expect from a bunch of superstitious hillbillies from the most backward state in the nation? Who still danced with poisonous snakes at church services, married their first cousins, and wore no shoes until they were old enough to vote?

Josh was from the big city. He was too sophisticated, too worldly, to believe in monsters or the supernatural.

Nonetheless, the creature's blood-chilling cry still seemed to ring in his ears even after the dense fog absorbed it into an eerie silence known only to the still Northwoods. Whatever it was clearly didn't want him here. Nobody would ever have to know he chickened out and ran. He wouldn't have to tell Elizabeth. Her old man had fought in Operation *Desert Storm* and claimed not to be afraid of Satan himself.

Josh could almost feel little red pig eyes glaring at him out of the fog like in *The Amityville Horror.* He vowed never to watch Saturday Night SyFy with Elizabeth again.

He made a complete circle in the trail, squinting against the cloud that trapped him in its clammy fist. His heart hammered. Right after he met Elizabeth he had solo-canoed across the Yukon Territory, down the Big Salmon River to the Yukon River and then over to Dawson City and Alaska. In the midnight sun he came across a ghost town called Fort Selkirk, in whose weed-choked graveyard he had felt unseen, ghostly eyes watching him.

He felt eyes like that watching him now.

What kind of an adventurer was he to be frightened off by footprints, the cry of an animal and his own active imagination? Nothing had otherwise changed. Somebody was hurt and in serious trouble. He wouldn't want to be abandoned if the situation were reversed. Besides, he had an unexplained feeling that his destiny lay at the end of the trail. What if Jack had never climbed that beanstalk?

He took another deep breath to calm and fortify himself. Knife in one hand, stout staff in the other, he took one step, another, avoiding the strange creature's footprint in the trail as if to step in it might transform him into the monster.

He climbed uphill into unknown territory. The cloud snugged tight around him, limiting his view to within a few feet all around, isolating him in silence so deep he felt he might be drowning in a murky pool of water. His courage rallied bit by bit as nothing further menaced him.

At another trail junction, one branch twisted around the mountain to the left while the other went right. Robert Frost might counsel for the less-traveled road, but someone seeking help would undoubtedly take the beaten path. That was the one Josh selected.

It seemed to circle the base of the mountain. The cloud thickened, restricting visibility even more. It was the kind of morning in which the cadence of the heart sounded like Apache drums.

He came to still another fork in the trail. Life was like that. Full of crooks, junctions and intersections. A man's fate depended upon the choices he made.

He took the left fork and began climbing steadily. Perhaps he would ascend above the clouds where he could see better. Instead, to his dismay, he encountered yet *another* Y. He made his choice based upon no particular logic. That trail soon grew faint. It twisted and looped and cut back on itself through forest so dense it consumed the sound of his beating heart and bellowing lungs.

He stopped to rest on a felled tree trunk. Not having intended to trek far, he had brought neither food nor water. His tongue felt like a cactus grown in parched soil. His stomach growled. To take his mind off these discomforts, he flashed his thoughts back to the dark apparition that crossed the trail in front of him and the outlandish print in the loam. It seemed of no species that he had ever seen or read about.

He looked for other sign as he hiked, but the soft soil of lower down turned into a kind of hard, loose glacial pebble not readily imprinted. Even his own fresh footfalls disappeared immediately, erased as thoroughly as though he had never traveled this way. Such was man's significance. Stick your hand in a bucket of water, Plato challenged, remove it and the water became as though it had never been disturbed. Or was that Confucius?

Josh had never felt so alone in his life. He *hoped* he was alone.

He rested on another felled tree for a long while, pondering, listening. Not even the twitter of a bird broke the quiet. He took out his cell phone. It had been dead from the time he left Victoria Island; it was still dead. What, he had expected to maybe punch in 911? *Come quick, I need help!*

Where are you?

Where indeed? *The Twilight Zone?*

He sighed, regained his feet and wearily started back the way he had come. He had *tried* to help, hadn't he? What else could he do?

At the next trail junction, he couldn't recall which path to take. Even Hansel and Gretel had marked their trail with bread crumbs. He got down on hands and knees to look for footprints to guide him. He thought he detected where weight had compressed the ground enough to make an impression. That must be the way back.

He followed that trail through another intersection, two forks and a Y before it dawned on him that he was walking in circles. The forest was a maze of game trails, all of which seemed to twist incestuously back into themselves.

Water and civilization always lay downhill. Josh took a downhill trail and made good time despite the fog and the trees clutching at his clothing like witches or trolls. After a mile or so, the trail dead-ended in undergrowth so thick he would have needed a bulldozer to get through. Disappointed, he began to retrace his steps.

Thirst became a real consideration. Hunger he could cope with, but the exertion of beating his way up and down hills and through forest was taking a toll. He developed a headache and felt queasy, first symptoms of hypothermia.

Remembering his survival techniques, he walked slowly looking for a hollow stump that might have collected rain water. He was hesitant about venturing too far off the trail lest he become disoriented and not find his way back. He sucked on mist-wet willow leaves, but they failed to quench his thirst. He was sweating furiously returning uphill, further dehydrating himself.

All he had to do was make it back to the stream where he found the boat. He should have known not to go into that basement.

Time seemed to compress around him. Hours passed while he wandered about in the maze and fog. He finally admitted he was lost again and collapsed onto a fallen log. He felt dizzy from thirst. The log was broad enough to allow him to stretch out and rest before he re-tackled the mission of finding his way out of this green hell.

He was so overcome with exhaustion that he drifted off and may have slumbered until nightfall had not a scream like the one before shattered the stillness like brittle crystal and jarred him instantly awake and to his feet. The fog had dissipated some while he slept, but it was still so thick he could see nothing either way along the trail.

Although a man not easily intimidated, he had been caught off-guard by everything that had transpired since he got lost days before. Add to that the tension of the bullet hole, the footprint, the screaming, getting lost again, and his nerves were frayed. The otherworldly scream that awoke him seemed to vibrate through his soul for long seconds after the fog absorbed the actual sound.

Then he heard footfalls pounding down the trail toward him. The first image that came to mind was the nut in *The Texas Chainsaw Massacre*. A knife and a staff were little defense against a chainsaw. He dived behind the fallen tree and peered over it into the fog.

Fog swirled. Out of it burst two dark-skinned men garbed in dirty flannel shirts, jeans and lumberjack boots. The skinny one wore a *Patriots* baseball cap; the other was bareheaded. Although both carried rifles, they looked more terrified than Josh felt. They shouted at each other in an Indian dialect he didn't understand. Heiltuk probably.

Without so much as missing a stride, the skinny Indian fired his rifle back over his shoulder into the fog. They disappeared down the trail into the cloud.

Softer, quicker footfalls followed. Josh ducked lower as a hairy dark form materialized out of vapor. The shape was too indistinct in the mist for Josh to identify, but he certainly would not have classified it as *Homo sapiens*.

It paused with the disturbed cloud roiling around it. It screamed again, breaking icicles down Josh's spine— and then it turned its shaggy head and looked directly into Josh's eyes.

Chapter Four

To his surprise, the beast's eyes glaring into his somehow lacked the impact they should have had. They looked more frightened than threatening, although the Indians hadn't stayed around long enough to notice. If it was the same creature he had glimpsed before in the fog, it looked so much smaller under direct scrutiny.

The eyes were soft and of a remarkable green, the broad face as expressionless and ill-formed as a mask. Since Josh had already been noticed, he decided on impulse to stand up and confront the menace, whatever its nature.

"Hey!" he exclaimed, like shouting at a stray dog.

The creature reacted like a stray dog. It turned tail and plunged back up the trail. Before it disappeared into the cloud, Josh noticed an improbable tag of blue cloth flapping from a rent in the animal's skin. This being, whatever it was, *whoever* it was, appeared more *E.T. The Extraterrestrial* than Mr. Hyde. Somebody in a big monkey suit.

"Wait up!" he shouted. "I won't hurt you."

He vaulted the log and chased recklessly after it. He heard rapid footfalls ahead. In the trail were monstrous footprints like the one he had seen before.

"Please wait!" he yelled.

Whatever it was, was *fast*. The sound of running grew faint and then vanished. Josh slowed his pace, caution having returned after his moment of foolhardiness. After all, the guy in that suit could be a slasher, the killer responsible for the bullet hole in the boat.

The trail led through forest that seemed to crouch in the mist, indistinct and ephemeral, dark and forbidding. A perfect setting for one of Elizabeth's horror flicks. Monster and all. Perhaps chasing it had not been his most prudent option.

The fog thinned somewhat as the trail climbed. Soon, he came to an opening in the woods and hesitated at what appeared to be the edge of a grassy clearing. He couldn't see all the way across in the gloom. Finally, against his better judgment, he ventured out of the forest and started warily across the glade.

The outline of a log cabin gradually materialized to block his way. He approached it, knife and staff ready for defense, his head twisting from side to side to catch forewarning of approaching danger. Who would possibly live out here away from everything? A half-wild hermit who shot trespassers and ground their bones to bake his bread? A human turned half-beast in animal skins?

"Hello the cabin!" he called out, the sudden sound of his own voice in the stillness causing him to cringe.

No answer. He came to a thick hand-hewn door. An overturned bucket lay to one side of the door while to the other a stack of firewood climbed halfway up the wall. He noticed an ax with its blade imbedded in a log. He thought to take it for a weapon. And perhaps a wooden stake as well. For all he knew, Dracula might be inside sleeping in his coffin.

Before he had the opportunity to either further arm himself or to knock on the door, the hairy shape from the trail sprang out from around a corner of the cabin, a rifle in its hands.

"I will shoot you," the beast promised. "I swear it. I'll shoot you like I did your friend."

Chapter Five

The creature's head was missing, in its place the head of a young woman set incongruously above broad hairy shoulders and a thick torso and legs also covered with hair. Josh regarded her with more curiosity than initial fear, in spite of the rifle pointed at him. Her face looked weathered and taut with tension below a mop of auburn hair tangled from recent neglect. The nose was long and thin above full sensuous lips compressed from stress. But the eyes were what caught his attention. They were of the most remarkable color. Bottle green with flecks of amber, filled with sadness. They were the *not* eyes of a monster.

She carried her monster's head tucked beneath her arm against her side while she leveled the rifle at Josh with both hands.

When nervous, Josh had a habit of speaking whatever came to mind. "Bride of Frankenstein, I presume?" he quipped. "Either that or I've missed a Halloween party."

"Party's over," she barked. She indicated his knife and staff with the barrel of her rifle. "Drop 'em."

He detected a flash of blue cloth where the top of the gorilla suit overlapped hairy trousers. As the expression on her face said she was not to be trifled with, Josh dropped his staff but further defied her order by returning his knife to its belt sheath. He held out empty palms toward her.

She was breathing hard from chasing Indians and then the run back, chased by Josh. An awful lot of chasing going on in the middle of nowhere.

Clearly, she wasn't sure what to do with him now that she had him captured. She didn't look as if she would grind his bones to make her bread.

"Now what?" Josh ventured to lighten the situation. "Play house?"

"Shut up. Let me think." Her accent was more American than Canadian. "Who are you? What are you doing here?"

He thought he had best cooperate. If there was anything more dangerous than a mama grizzly, it was a lady suffering PMS while holding a rifle.

"I'm a stranger in an even stranger land," he replied, glancing at the fake head underneath her arm. "I have no idea what's going on here, why you were chasing those men pretending to be a werewolf—"

"Sasquatch," she corrected him.

"Obviously a mighty effective one, judging from the looks on their faces."

"Indians in Canada are superstitious. They believe in the old legends of wild men in the forest."

"And wild *women*, I assume. Look, I'm not with them. I saw blood in the boat—"

Her face paled through its weathering. "Blood. . .?"

"I thought someone was hurt and needed help."

"I—I..." Her voice trailed off into a horrified whisper. She recovered quickly. "You are all trying to kill me," she accused. "I'll shoot you too, if I have to."

She jabbed the rifle at him. A *paranoid* lady on PMS with a rifle.

"You won't have to, miss. I'm simply relieved you carry your *other* head under your arm."

She wasn't amused. She might actually be more frightened than he.

"I was kayaking and got lost," he explained. "But you already know that, don't you? You were watching me yesterday when I found the boat."

Her expression said she didn't know what he was talking about. He changed tact.

"Miss, what are you doing out here? Are you alone?"

"Not as alone as I would like," she said.

He thought the crisis moment had passed when she might actually shoot him with little provocation. But she was still one dangerous female. A *frightened* paranoid lady on PMS with a rifle. And, oh, yes. Wearing a Sasquatch outfit.

Her apparent indecision offered Josh some encouragement. "I hate to break up the party just as it gets going," he said. "But I'm afraid I left my costume in

Seattle. So, if you'll lower your weapon I'll be on my merry way."

She stiffened. "No."

"No?"

"Yes."

"Is it yes or no?"

"Yes, it's no."

"No's on first base."

She looked at him as though *he* were the one who was crazy. He figured maybe he'd better cool it with the wisecracks. She was obviously in no mood for it. Considering the blood in the boat, her mood could only get worse. This was turning into *Pumpkin Head.*

"I can't let you go," she declared, making up her mind. She gestured with the rifle and moved toward him in her ridiculous hair suit. "Open the door and go inside."

"Finally, the celebrated Canadian hospitality."

"Just shut up and do as you're told."

"You're sounding more and more like Elizabeth."

He opened the unlocked cabin door and stepped inside. She paused in the doorway behind him to look all around the clearing, as though searching for his accomplices. She slammed the door and dropped down a heavy bar.

The cabin was small, with only two rooms. The larger in which he found himself served as a combination living room and kitchen. Through an interior opening, he saw a bed covered in thick handmade quilts. A single window beyond a crude wooden dining table with matching crude chairs barely squeezed in enough light to soften the darkness. He hesitated to let his eyes adjust.

She poked him in the back. "Sit in the chair," she ordered, poking him some more toward a straight-backed chair placed near a pot-bellied wood stove. He eased down on the chair.

"Put your hands behind your back."

He leaned forward. She stepped back, snapping the rifle to a more threatening position.

"Easy, miss. Easy."

"Hands *behind* the chair back," she amended.

He did so. He faced an oil cooking stove below some rough, open cupboards on the opposite side of the room. Dishes, plates and cups were visible on the shelves while iron skillets and pots hung from nails on the wall. She kept the rifle trained on him with one hand while she fetched a coil of cotton rope from a wooden box. She circled behind him and pecked him on the back of the head with the muzzle of her weapon to let him know she meant business.

"I'll shoot if you try anything."

"I believe you."

A loop of rope snatched his wrists. As quickly as that, she bound his hands so snugly behind the chair back that he was afraid he would lose circulation in them. She next secured his feet to the lower chair rung and stepped back, satisfied. Trussed up like a goat at a goat roping.

"Kinky," he murmured.

While he watched, she skinned off the Sasquatch suit. It was padded with old clothes and quilts to make her appear bulkier than she actually was. Underneath all that, she was slender and well-built in faded blue jeans and a red-and-green flannel shirt. She dragged over another chair and sat on it opposite him while she removed the enormous shoe-feet with which she had made tracks on the trails. He was surprised she could have run so fast with the big wooden soles, the suit and all its padding.

That accomplished, she leaned back with the rifle resting across her thighs and released a weary sigh.

"Now what?" Josh asked.

"I still might have to shoot you if your friends come back."

Chapter Six

Had Josh been a praying man, he would have immediately offered a prayer that his "friends" stayed away while this crazy girl who thought she was a Sasquatch was holding a gun on him.

"I seem to be at a disadvantage," he pointed out.

She looked at him. He had never seen eyes so green and full of shadows, highlights and mystery. She stood up suddenly and went to the window to peek out, standing to one side so she would not be seen by any observer on the outside. She ducked underneath the window level to the other side to look out again. It was twilight by now, which meant around ten p.m. this time of year. It was getting so dark inside he could barely make out her form across the room. He had napped longer on that log than he had intended.

"My name is Josh Logan," he offered.

She ignored him. It was as if he ceased to exist once she had rendered him helpless. The crazy woman in *Misery* broke her captive's legs with a baseball bat so he couldn't get away.

She went to the cupboard and scrounged around in it with one hand, holding onto her weapon with the other. She stepped back, looking disappointed. Then she knelt and opened the lid of a larder and took from it a handful of jerky. She returned to sit in the chair as before while she chewed on a piece. Josh's parched throat and grumbling belly reminded him that he had had nothing to eat or drink since ham 'n eggs this morning.

"You always eat alone?" he asked, hoping she took the hint.

She hesitated, then broke off a chunk of the dried meat, got up, and shoved it at his face from as far back as she could still reach him. He popped open his mouth to avoid being stabbed. He chewed while she resumed her vigil, but his mouth was so dry he choked and began coughing violently.

"Water?"

She brought him a tin cup of tepid water from a red gas container. She waited until he stopped coughing before letting him drink. He drained the cup with her help.

"More," he pleaded.

She let him drink another cup full. He felt much better, except his hands were growing numb.

She stood in front of him wearing a scowl. "Why are you trying to murder me?" she demanded bluntly.

"Right. *You're* the aggrieved party here," he retorted. "Why are you running around in a gorilla suit scaring Indians?"

"Sasquatch," she corrected him again.

This had gone on long enough. "What's the difference?" he snapped.

"There are no gorillas in Canada."

"And there *are* Sasquatch?"

"*Ba'oush. Boq. Dsonoqua.* They are known by many names to all the tribes of North America."

"At least we're making progress," he marveled. "Proving that you *do* understand the fundamentals of conversation."

"Don't be a wise ass. I'm the one with the gun."

That jarred him back into place. This was no singles bar in Chicago where men and women met and entertained each other with clever repartee while they jockeyed for a suitable outcome. Josh recalled that it had been in such a place, *Cloud Nine*, that he had hooked up with Elizabeth. A one-nighter with a spoiled rich girl led to Saturday Night SyFy, an engagement ring, and a prospective partnership with her old man.

He wondered about the outcome of *this* encounter.

"Perhaps we've gotten off to a bad start," he said. "What say we start over? My name is Josh Logan. What's yours?"

She studied him. Her eyes looked hooded, guarded. He bobbed his head to prompt her.

Finally, she answered, cautiously. "Chaya."

"Now we're making progress, Chaya. You're not Canadian?"

"Like you didn't know," she accused.

"How could I have known?"

She rose and took another look out the window at the encroaching night. She walked with a lithe grace. Like the girl in the old movie who changed back and forth from panther to human, who in her feline mode went out to stalk and kill. Elizabeth liked vampires, but she liked the panther-girl too.

Chaya returned and sat down across from him. He could barely make out the outline of her face.

"Let's go back to the gorilla outfit. . . Pardon. *Sasquatch*."

She looked at him; he couldn't quite discern the frown on her face but it was evident in the tilt of her head. She clasped a hand over one knee, the rifle still resting across her jeaned thighs. The wedding ring on her finger picked up a dying glint of light from the window. He thought of the blood and bullet hole in the boat.

"Where's your husband. . .?"

"I didn't shoot *him,* if that's what you're implying."

This was becoming *The Shining*. With the ax outside the door.

"Well, I didn't!" she snapped.

"Anything you say. You're the one with the gun. How about turning on some lights?"

"*No!* Answer *my* question," she insisted. "Why are you and the Indians trying to kill me?"

"I don't know what the hell you're talking about."

"You expect me to believe you just wandered in here all on your own?"

"You expected me to believe that you're a Sasquatch."

They glared at each other. It occurred to Josh that confrontation might not be his most reasonable approach. She glanced toward the window. He thought he saw her shiver. Unspeakable *things* crept around in darkness. She returned her attention to him.

"He'll be back, probably tonight," she said. "He's big and he won't be happy at what you've done."

"Who?"

"You asked about my husband. George."

"Where did he go?"

Again, the puzzled tilt of her head. "You really don't know?"

"I've been trying to tell you. I didn't do whatever I'm supposed to have done."

She appeared to consider it. "Huh!" she snorted. "Like I'm going to believe any man at face value."

She considered it some more.

"He left three days ago in our boat to pick up supplies at Hartley Bay. That's when the Indians showed up. Them and another man. I don't know what happened to him."

"You shot him," Josh suggested, trying not to sound accusing.

"And then *you* took his place." *She* sounded accusing.

"Chaya, my life is so screwed up I can barely take my own place."

He knew she still didn't believe him.

"Look," he reasoned, "if what you say is true and they're trying to murder you, they'll be back if we stay here. They'll know where you live."

For the first time he recognized the crack in the veneer of her protective attitude. "I—I have nowhere else to go," she faltered. "So far, I've kept them scared off. I don't understand why they're doing this. Look around. George and I— We have nothing anybody could possibly want. What you see is it. You can have this old cabin if you want it. George and I will build another."

What could he do to get it through her head that she had nothing he wanted?

"Untie me," he offered. "Maybe I can help."

"I can't do that, mister."

"Chaya, my name is Josh."

You named something, you weren't so easily willing to destroy it. He had to convince her that he meant her no harm. Otherwise, he and Jamie Curtis were already in the basement, looking at the moldy coffin.

He stiffened at a rustling sound that came from the dark behind the cabin. Chaya sprang to her feet. Suddenly came the reek of spilled gasoline, followed by a whoosh like air released into space from a punctured balloon. Tongues of flame instantly licked at the single window. Josh's first panicked thought was that the cabin would go up like a torched cardboard box.

"*Untie me!*"

Instead, she emitted a cry sharp enough to petrify the living dead, snatched up her gorilla suit and other head, and ran out of the cabin with her rifle, slamming the door behind her.

"*Don't leave me like this!*" he shouted, but she had already done just that. Left him bound in the middle of what would become a raging inferno within a very few minutes.

Chapter Seven

He had to get to the door and outside before flames enveloped the cabin. He wrestled with his restraints, twisting and tugging. He shouted Chaya's name.

"*Damn you, bitch!*"

Using his toes for balance, he rocked back and forth, frantically trying to "walk" the chair to the door. Panic lodged in his throat. Dragons were on the way. Smoke-acid tears spilled from his eyes. Coughing and gagging and spitting, yelling the bitch's name, jumping the chair. Making a few inches progress.

He had once read about a wildfire traveling so fast through Gambol oak in Colorado that it burned a squirrel to death in full flight. That was how swiftly fire could eat its way through dry timber—or through an old log cabin.

He was not going to make it.

Smoke was so thick he could barely *see* the door. Coughing was robbing him of his strength. Flames gnawed at the cupboards, crept across the floor toward him.

He continued to struggle. He had the chair bouncing. Then he lost his balance. The chair teetered precariously on one leg before it, and he with it, crashed to the floor.

"*Oh, God, no!*"

Elizabeth would never forgive him.

He lay on his side, no longer able to use even his toes. The air tasted fresher close to the floor. It revived him, a little. He caught his breath. In renewed hope, he threw his weight from side to side within the diminished parameters of his tethers, trying to again bounce toward the door.

In sparring with the floor and the chair, he inadvertently flipped himself onto his back, an even more hopeless position, if that were possible at this stage. He screamed as his weight crushed his hands and arms between the floor and the chair back. He was left staring up at the cedar shake roof in horror, as helpless as a turtle upside down on its shell.

Tiny spittles of flame scabbed at the wooden shingles, tonguing through, huffing lungfuls of smoke. In a few more minutes the inferno would consume the cabin and collapse the burning roof on top of him. Lo, squirrel caught, although not exactly in full flight.

No one would look for him in this wilderness. Myths would spring up around his disappearance. Sometimes when he watched blood-and-gore with Elizabeth, he contemplated how he might die. He never thought it would end like this. He wondered who would watch Saturday Night SyFy with Elizabeth now.

Sparks shattered from a wad of shingles falling to the floor nearby. He cried out.

He was a goner. Exhausted from his struggles, coughing violently, he was about to accept his fate when the door suddenly banged open, venting smoke and superheated air like a chimney. Into the swirl appeared the surreal, indistinct form of Chaya as Josh had first seen her—in full Sasquatch outfit, including the head. Out scaring the Indians again. He called out to her in relief. She said nothing. Simply dropped on her knees next to him and pushed the chair over onto its side so she could get to his hands.

She fumbled with his bonds. His consciousness seemed as ephemeral as the smoke that engulfed them. Like a nightmare during which the threat approached while you were paralyzed and unable to do anything about it.

One hand broke free. Chaya-Sasquatch switched attention to his feet. She was working on them while Josh finished freeing his hands. Firebrands from the roof showered onto her bent back. Her gorilla suit flared up like a torch. She screamed in alarm and, suddenly, she was thrashing around on the floor trying to put out the flames and get out of her costume. Like the dying throes of the scarecrow in *Children of the Corn*.

Chapter Eight

Josh had enough left in him to quickly free his feet. He tumbled away from the chair toward where Chaya was rolling about like a screaming ball of fire. Like *Pumpkinhead* when *his* cabin went up in flames. Ignoring his survival instincts, he ripped off his flannel shirt and used it to beat out the blazes that engulfed Chaya's monkey suit. After all, she *had* returned for him at great peril to her own life.

The tough bear skin from which she had fashioned the getup was the only thing that saved her. He succeeded in extinguishing the burning hair, by which time she had either fainted or passed out from smoke inhalation. Still coughing violently, he lurched to his feet and dragged her across the floor ahead of the fire and out the door where night had pressed the last red wine out of twilight.

Flames illuminated the edges of the surrounding forest. Menacing shadows like ghouls or active zombies skittered about among the trees, leaping and threatening in rampage against the escape of those who should have been a certain sacrifice to chaos. Even though Chaya had rushed out with her monkey suit to chase off the Indians who presumably had set the fire, Josh couldn't help being acutely aware that the sadistic pyros who had doused the cabin in gasoline might nonetheless be watching from the darkness. He felt naked and exposed and vulnerable in the firelight.

On the grass lay the rifle where Chaya dropped it when she came back for him. He scooped it up. Although debilitated by heat and smoke, coughing so hard he could hardly catch his breath, he dragged

Chaya into the woods and away from the burning cabin. He tore off her smoldering gorilla-Sasquatch disguise and cast it aside before he left her lying on the moss and collapsed with his back against a forest giant tree.

She stank of burnt hair and wood smoke. Josh suppressed his wheezing out of fear of attracting their assailants, but Chaya had no such caution as she began to revive. She appeared not seriously injured. He was also in reasonably good shape, considering what they had survived. Only his hands suffered burns from fighting out the fire that almost took her life. He flexed his fingers and felt the searing pain. He suspected blisters would form, but he probably wouldn't have deep scars. He could still use a gun or a kayak paddle.

He moved a few feet away from Chaya to keep watch with the rifle while she struggled back to life. There was little he could do to shush her in her half-conscious state. Away from the heat of the fire, he shivered in his t-shirt from the night cool and from the desperate realization of their plight.

Somebody really *was* attempting to murder her. Whoever it was, and for whatever motive, would also have to kill him. He had gone down into the basement and there seemed to be no way out.

Chapter Nine

He heard her slowly coming around to full awareness, arms thrashing, legs scratching the floor of the forest like fingernails at the window in *Salem's Lot*. *Let me in, let me in.*

He resisted the urge to clasp his hands over her mouth and tell her to shut up. That would probably only make things worse. All he wanted right now was for her to get on her feet so they could flee the body snatchers with the speed of Road Runner in the cartoons. *Beep! Beep!*

While he waited for her, he made himself small and hopefully invisible against the bole of the giant fir, rifle across his lap. He strained his ears for sounds that might indicate the return of their attackers. He noticed how he was beginning to use the plural possessive. *Our* attackers.

The night was as quiet as an abandoned church. The fog had dissipated and the silence of the stars filled the heavens.

Quiet. Yeah, too quiet.

Chaya stopped moving about. He waited. He *felt* her sit up and look around. He slapped the rifle softly with his palm to let her know what it was and where he was.

"I'm the one with the gun now," he whispered.

After a few moments, she reacquired her bearings and said, "It doesn't have any bullets."

"You captured me with an unloaded rifle!"

"He took all the shells."

"George?"

"Who else?"

"Why would he leave you with no means of defense?"

"I found two cartridges he overlooked at the bottom of an old backpack."

"With which you promptly shot up your husband and his boat."

"I told you it *wasn't* George."

He didn't know what to believe. Hand cupped over the rifle's ejection port, he quickly bolted open the chamber to check the magazine. Empty. That explained the basic black-in-Sasquatch outfit—her last line of defense.

"You saved my life," she murmured reluctantly.

"You saved mine first. After you damned near got me killed."

"I thought you were—"

He sighed. "I know what you thought."

"I'm sorry. Josh, I really mean it."

He said back her name. "Chaya."

Knowing names somehow bound you to each other.

They couldn't stay here. Sooner or later, as soon as the cabin burned down to coals and ashes, whoever tried to kill them would most likely return to check the results. This wasn't Chicago where you could depend on cops and firefighters to come with sirens blaring to scurry about the crime scene playing *NCIS*.

A thought occurred to him. "Did you see anyone when you ran out of the cabin? Do you think they saw you?"

"I heard them running away in the dark."

"Good. Maybe they'll think we went up in flames."

He stood up. He thought about discarding the useless rifle, but decided to hang on to it. It might at least serve as an anchor.

"Your place or mine?" he quipped. "Oh, I forgot. You don't have a place anymore."

"What are we going to do?"

"FBI Witness Protection Program?"

He saw a shifting of shadows made by firelight filtering through trees as she stood up in front of him. She emitted a tiny cry of pain. He reached to steady her.

"Are you all right?"

"Bruises, maybe singed around the edges a little. You?"

"Same. Mostly my hands. But it's better than being fricasseed. Do you think you can guide us in the dark back to where I beached my kayak and made camp? I was lost when I stumbled across you. It's near the mouth of the creek. We can hide out there and maybe get some sleep before daylight—after you explain what all the *Dungeons and Dragons* is about. Agreed?"

"You'll have to give me your hand so we don't get separated."

They found each other's hands. Her hand was dry, rough and calloused. Elizabeth's hands were soft and always moisturized. Chaya squeezed his hand to let him know they had to trust each other. He winced from the pain. She remained still and silent and he realized she was looking through the timber toward the glow of her burning home. Words could not have conveyed her sense of loss more than that look.

"We'd better go," she said.

There was, he thought, only the two of them against the odds.

Chapter Ten

Chaya had a splendid sense of direction and place, plus this *was* her home territory. With the aid of stars and a quarter-moon rising, she led Josh to the creek below the abandoned boat and thus downstream to the channel. They kept conversation to a minimum. Josh doubted their enemies would be out roaming in such darkness, but it was best to not take chances.

She held onto his hand for reassurance. He submitted willingly, even though his palms were tender from the fire burn. The physical contact was as comforting to him as it seemed to be to her after the dreadful events of the day. He initially thought her tough and hard enough to crack walnuts with her thighs. He wasn't so sure of that now. He detected a certain feminine vulnerability in her manner that was both off-putting and attractive.

He had never met a girl like her in Chicago. Elizabeth's idea of roughing it was a Waldorf-Astoria in Orlando.

The little creek made sluggish black water purls in the wan moonlight where it merged into the outgoing tide of the channel. Still holding hands, they worked around the inlet to where Josh tethered his kayak the previous afternoon. Had it only been a little over twenty four hours ago that *The Creature from the Black Lagoon* began?

Diurnal tides in this part of the world reached to thirty feet, resulting in steep rocky shorelines and mazes of washed-up tree trunks and brush. Josh strained his eyes through the ambient light to pick out his kayak from the ground clutter. The bright yellow of the slender little craft should have been easy to see. It was nowhere in sight.

Alarmed, they crouched in the darkness, hardly daring to breathe, hearing only the soft lapping of the receding tide against the beach. An owl up the hill inquired of another.

Observing nothing that seemed out of place, but nonetheless cautious, Josh took the lead and approached the huge roots of a felled tree to which he had tethered the kayak on a long line to prevent its being swamped by high tides. Feeling around, he found the knot then followed the rope hand over hand to where last night's tide deposited the boat in a drift.

"Can we use it to escape?" Chaya whispered.

"*One* of us can."

He felt her stiffen.

"Don't get your panties in a twist. It'll only seat one person. We'll have to think of something else—and not another Sasquatch."

"I was desperate." She gave his hand a reprimanding squeeze.

"Ouch!"

"Sorry. I forgot."

He scrambled into the drift and dragged the kayak into a hollow of logs above the high tide mark where it would not be readily spotted. He returned to her with a thought.

"The gas can in the boat was empty."

"I wouldn't still be here if it had had gas."

"Is it your husband's boat?"
"George has a Kris Kraft."
"Whoever burned your cabin—"
"—the Indians—"
"—must have more gas. Obviously, they're not using that boat after you put a bullet in it."

They were talking while standing directly in front of each other so their voices wouldn't carry. Her head nodded against his chest. She was falling asleep on her feet.

"I've barely slept in three nights," she apologized.
"Come on. You can use my sleeping bag."
She hesitated.
"Without me in it," he added. "I'll keep watch."
"Do you have a firearm?"
"No, but I saw *Predator* three times."

Chapter Eleven

They climbed off the beach past deadfalls into the deeper darkness of conifer forest. As they groped around for the tent, something attacked with arms and legs silhouetted against a patch of stars visible through an opening in the trees. Chaya jumped back with a muffled shriek, stumbled over Josh and fell. He took a knee next to her.

"No, no," he said quickly. "It's my scare-bear."
Her breath continued to come in gasps.
"I hung up my wetsuit to scare off bears," he further explained. "I thought I saw one yesterday by the creek."
She finally caught her breath. "It stinks. Does it work?"
"Better than a Sasquatch."
She shifted positions to better see the scare-bear against stars. "You really are weird," she said.
"That's what my fiancée says."

He patted her shoulder before he crawled into his tent on all fours and directed her inside after him. He left the flap open. Not that he actually expected to see anything in the dark, but he still didn't like the idea of being cornered without an escape route. He had rather suffer the black flies and mosquitoes.

"We'll be safe here until daybreak," he surmised. "You saw how hard it was for us to find the tent—and we *knew* where it was. We'll hear them coming a mile away."

"And then, after daybreak, what?" she whispered.

"Vampires can't stand the sunlight."

"Your fiancée is right. You are weird."

"Just an All-American boy. I won't bite your neck. Here..." He directed her hand to the opening in his sleeping bag. "It smells better than scare-bear. Not much, but you need your sleep."

"What about you?"

"I had a nap today on a log before two Indians and a girl wearing a bearskin disturbed me."

She couldn't suppress a giggle at the impression that must have made. She fumbled around and wriggled gratefully into the bag while he went through his pack to find a First Aid kid. He heard the bag zip up. He opened a tin of ointment.

"What's that?" she asked.

"For my hands. Do you need doctoring?"

"I've played doctor before, when I was a kid." She sat up. "Here, let me do it." She felt for the tin in his hand. "Hold out your palms."

He did. She tenderly massaged in the salve.

"Feels better already," he said. "Do you need it?"

"I'm okay, thanks to you. Josh? What's your fiancée's name?"

"Elizabeth, most of the time."

"And the rest of the time?"

"Ma'am. As in, Yes, Ma'am."

"You're marrying a Yes, Ma'am?"

"I thought you were sleepy."

"I am. When are you getting married?"

"When I get back to Chicago." He returned the ointment to his pack. "If I make it back," he added.

"Do you love her?"

"Isn't that what marriage is about?"

"Not always."

"Do you love George?"

He thought it significant that she didn't reply right away. Maybe she had dozed off. Finally, she sighed softly. "I did. Once. I think."

"What happened?"

They spoke in such low tones that Josh had to lie down next to the sleeping bag so they could talk without raising their voices.

"You're right," she said. "I'm not Canadian. I'm from the cornfields of Iowa. I met George when we were students at the University of Wisconsin. He was from British Columbia."

Once she started, she didn't seem able to stop.

"Same old story from time immemorial. Girl meets boy. Boy sweeps girl off her feet. Girl follows boy onto the frontier to build a life, raise cabbages, chickens and kids, shoot moose, catch halibut and chop firewood. You've heard it before."

"Not quite like that."

"That was seven years ago. I do actually love it here. Where you can see God when you speak to Him. It's like the earth is a cathedral and nature has her arms open to accept you for what you are."

She turned onto her side to face him. They couldn't see each other in the dark, but her breath was warm and naturally sweet in his nostrils. Elizabeth's breath always smelled of mints.

"Somehow things got cold between George and me," she continued presently. "He began to leave me alone here for longer and longer periods. You know something? After awhile, I didn't really mind. I didn't care if he came back or not if I'd only had a boat so I could go to the trading post for supplies."

"Why did he leave this time?"

"He got in the Kris Kraft and left three days ago. Told me it wasn't any of my business where he went."

"And about that same time—"

"*They* showed up. The same afternoon. I was up on the hill above the creek where we have a vegetable garden. I saw a boat creeping upstream in the creek. A guy got out—a white man, not an Indian. So I went down to meet him. I thought something had happened to George. Out here, there are so few of us that we have little reason to be suspicious."

"You don't trust your doctor or the cop on the corner in Chicago."

"That's one of the reasons I came to Canada with George."

"This guy that came up? He the one you shot?"

"I didn't want to, Josh." Her voice went husky with underlying tears. She moved closer. Their bodies curved together through the sleeping bag. She was trembling.

"He grabbed me when I came up to him," she went on. "He had a grizzly foot and he tried to rip open my throat with the claws. I fought him as hard as I could. He missed my throat but cut my shoulder. I kneed him. . . Well, you know where. I ran. He chased me, yelling and cursing, but I beat him back to the garden where I left my rifle. I told you I had two shells.

"He kept coming, even when I aimed the rifle at him and told him I'd shoot. He didn't believe me. He kind of sneered and said, 'It ain't loaded.' How would he have known that?"

"I *believed* you," Josh interjected, "even though it wasn't loaded."

"You should have seen the surprised look on his face when I shot him. He ran back to his boat. I thought he was going to get a gun and come back. He dived into the boat and I took my last shot. I could tell he was hurt bad, but he pushed off."

Josh heard the catch in her throat.

"I was so scared," she admitted. "The next day the tide washed up his boat. I checked it. It was out of gas. I guess you saw the bullet hole and the blood. The Indians must have taken his gas. They showed up the same afternoon. The first thing they tried to do was break into the cabin. I bluffed them. They didn't know if I had anymore shells or not."

"You didn't, so you turned Sasquatch?"

"We had this bearskin rug. I sewed a costume with a head and big feet. It worked at first. That was about when you showed up. I thought you were with them."

"Something I don't understand," Josh mused. "If they wanted to murder you, why didn't they just shoot you and get it over with?"

He tasted her breath fresh in his face.

"I found something," she said.

He waited. This seemed hard for her.

"We've had a grizzly marauding around the cabin since the salmon runs started. It made no sense why George wouldn't leave a box of rifle shells for me. I was looking for more cartridges in a wooden box where George keeps his pack, skinning knives, fishing tackle and the like. I'll show you what I found when it gets light. I think you'll understand then."

"I think I'm beginning to."

"It all started falling together—why the intruder thought my rifle was empty, why he was trying to make it look like a bear got me—"

"Or that you burned up in a fire."

"I didn't want to believe it at first. What I found was an insurance policy on my life with George as beneficiary. There was a double indemnity clause that paid double if I died by accident. Life insurance policies don't pay off on murder or suicide. A bullet would have been suspicious."

Her voice hardened.

"My husband wants me dead," she concluded bitterly. "I'm worth a million dollars if he comes back and finds I've had an accident."

A chill twittered up Josh's spine. He listened for sounds in the darkness outside the tent, half-expecting George to turn up like Jack Nicholson in *The Shining*. "*I'm ba-a-a-ack!*" He didn't sound like the kind of guy who would be frightened off by big footprints, an empty rifle, or a Chicago city slicker who ignored all the warnings and went down into the basement.

Chapter Twelve

She slept then, snuggled up to him as close as the sleeping bag permitted. Josh's mind was too busy to have permitted slumber even had his body been inclined. Everything was running on overdrive—and it was exciting. He was having the greatest adventure of his life. The strange and enticing woman next to him, the danger, the raw primitiveness combined to make him feel more truly alive than ever before. Win or lose, this was how life was supposed to be, not stuck folded, spindled and mutilated in a glass-paneled office behind a desk.

Elizabeth would have fallen apart in such a predicament, out of her element of gated communities, cops and cell phones. But with Chaya, this virtual stranger Chaya, it was she and he standing shoulder to shoulder against *Invaders from Outer Space*.

He woke her when the sky turned gray. Cloud cover hung low over the mountains, making fog. The air reeked of ozone and oncoming rain. He yawned.

"You didn't sleep," she said.

"Maybe tonight."

They shared freeze-dried spaghetti from his stash and went separate ways in the trees to relieve themselves. Morning ablutions completed, they sat on a felled tree trunk to ponder options and wait for traveling light to penetrate the fog. Chaya seemed in a much more positive frame of mind, especially considering how close they had come to being burned alive. Not being alone when trouble came improved a person's outlook.

"I'm glad you got lost," she said. She had a wonderful smile.

He grinned back. "I'm glad you aren't."

"Does that mean we're not lost if we're together?"

He didn't know what he should read into that, so he changed the subject. "I've been thinking. We can't walk out, we can't use the kayak, and the boat we do have is out of gas. If you're right about your husband, he may have dropped off the Indians—or *they* have another boat."

"I'm sure they'll offer to drive us to Bella Bella," she replied with a sarcastic half-smile, adding, "Josh, they have guns."

"They won't use them because of the life insurance."

"They can shoot you."

"Good point. I'd better stay close to you."

With sudden playfulness, she moved near him on the log and threw an arm over his shoulders. "This close?"

His heart jumped at her touch. He thought of Elizabeth and sobered.

"They have to complete what they started," he reasoned. "They can't let either of us live to testify against them. But they'll be cautious. George apparently thought he took all the rifle cartridges with him. They won't know if you have any left or not."

"Maybe they'll think you also have a gun."

"A bluff will only go so far. Where's the most likely place to moor a boat, other than the stream?"

"That'll be on the other side of the peninsula. About a mile. There's a trail."

He rose from the log, went to the tent and scrounged through his pack for a shirt to replace the one destroyed when he beat out Chaya's flames. She followed him and watched as he put it on over his t-shirt and tucked the tail into his jeans. This one was solid green.

"If we're lucky," he said, "they'll be sorting through the ashes at the cabin to make sure your body is there. While they're thus occupied, we steal their boat—and you and I are outa here."

"Back to Elizabeth?" she said.

He hesitated. "What will you do?"

He expected to see grief or sorrow expressed on her face. Instead, she merely looked resigned, overcome by a certain sadness. Her gaze shifted pensively in the direction where her home and everything she owned had burned to the ground.

"We'll have to watch out," she said. "I've seen the grizzly several times on the trail. She's a big sow with a yearling cub. That makes her a mean ol' bitch."

More to relieve tension with levity than in demonstration of any practical defense, Josh jumped back like a ninja warrior and slashed his arms about, startling Chaya.

"When I was a kid," he said, "Dad said I was so ugly I could hunt bears with a switch."

"You're not ugly, Josh."

"Dad had to tie a hundred dollar bill around my neck so I could get a date."

In what seemed like an impulse to him, she took a step forward and reached her palm to cradle the whiskered line of his jaw. Without saying a word, she rose on tiptoes to kiss him softly on the mouth. Then she jumped back as if from a spark. Neither of them knew how to respond. They stared at each other for a long breathtaking moment.

He turned away first, flustered. "It's getting daylight. Are you ready? To go, I mean."

She still regarded him, as though taken aback by her impetuosity.

"You'll have to lead the way," he added, still avoiding her eyes.

She turned carrying the rifle and started off through the woods, striding swiftly and with the grace of some young forest creature.

Chapter Thirteen

Josh had watched Stephen King's TV series *The Stand* three times with Elizabeth. "*M-o-o-n. That's how you spell Kansas.*" The hero played by Gary Sinese delivered a pivotal speech in which he proclaimed that there came a time when a man had to stand up against evil. It thrilled Josh and brought tears to his eyes each time he heard it. He never thought he would ever have to make such a dramatic commitment. But here he was off on a knight's errand to stand up against evil, slay the dragon and save the princess.

Well, not exactly a dragon. Nor a princess. But Chaya, he thought, possessed the qualities of a princess, certainly more so than any girl he had met in Chicago.

Including Elizabeth?

Perhaps he should have made a speech like Gary's before they set off: "It is an undertaking from which all might not return..."

Chaya paused to look back at him when the enveloping clouds began to leak a steady drizzle that pattered on leaves and dripped with a sound like slow blood. Her bottle green eyes were calm and trusting. He must let no doubt show in his own that would give her pause. He nodded and smiled. Rain would mask any sounds they made and help conceal them when the time came to act.

He couldn't help thinking of the *things* that lived in *The Mist*.

More by instinct than sight, Josh suspected, Chaya found a trail that circled low around the hills. She might have used the channel as a navigation aid except for the fog that cloaked it from view. Clouds that soaked them to the skin and made them shiver also cut visibility to near nothing. Sometimes Josh even lost sight of Chaya in slow gray whirlpools, and she was only a few steps ahead of him.

The wet crack of a tree branch nearby, as though beneath weight, froze them in place while they struggled to control chattering teeth and breath agitated by tension. The fog a mere ten feet ahead parted briefly as something or someone moved through it. A dark figure appeared and then instantly disappeared, swallowed back into the mist, leaving as its only evidence of presence the lingering stench of rotted salmon and the receding rush of its big body breaking through timber.

It left Josh stunned and speechless. He might have thought of Chaya and her bear suit, except she was right next to him and the fire had destroyed her Halloween costume.

Chaya found her voice. "The grizzly."

"Big," he croaked.

They continued, more cautiously than before. When they stopped to rest, he offered her his canteen. She took it, opened the cap but did not drink right away.

"Indian legend says that anyone who sees Bigfoot will have bad luck," she said unexpectedly. "Just before World War II, an Indian family named Chapman lived near here in a town called Ruby Creek. George, his wife Jeannie, and their three young children. Two boys and a girl. A Sasquatch busted into their cabin and tore it apart. The Chapmans escaped, but they had *seen* it. That was all it took. The three Chapman kids died within three years, the two boys from drowning and the little girl of a disease. George and Jeannie drowned a few years later."

"Now who's being superstitious?" he asked.

Chaya nodded. She took a drink. "It was a bear."

Chapter Fourteen

It was primitive country. They might have been living in *King Kong*. They were surrounded by tribal enemies and giant bears, apes, or whatever. The only thing a man could depend on in a crisis was himself, rather a novel idea to a guy from the big city. Even when Josh was mugged in Chicago, he knew all he had to do was hand over his wallet and then turn to the cops to take care of it. Out here, he *was* the cop. Along with his trusty green-eyed sidekick, whose previous persona had been that of a Chewbacca-like Sasquatch.

He grinned to himself in spite of the cold rain that had his teeth chattering and the prospect of extreme danger before the morning was out.

Chaya grew more cautious as the soggy trail lapped downhill toward the channel. Josh assumed they were drawing near where the Indians may have moored their boat. She halted and knelt close in the trail with him.

"There's a protected inlet cut between two boulders," she whispered. "The water's deep enough to tie up in, even at low tide. This trail and another from the cabin—rather, what *used* to be the cabin—lead to it."

Their faces were near enough to taste each other's breath.

"Josh, you don't have to do this. It can be dangerous."

He shrugged it off, although his heart was clearly pounding. "What kind of hero would I be if I abandoned the princess after she kissed me?"

She blushed and, at the same time, exhaled a sigh of relief.

After another ten minutes of cautious downhill travel, they came out on a high bluff. The tide was coming in again below as stealthily as the murderous orangutan in Edgar Allan Poe's *The Murder in the Rue Morgue*. Fog hid the channel from view, however, until an errant breeze kicked up from out at sea and parted the mist. Josh dropped to the ground and pulled Chaya down with him.

Not thirty feet ahead rose the twin boulders guarding the narrow mouth to the inlet. Almost immediately, a veil of gray rain returned to mask further scrutiny. The sound of voices, partly muffled, came from the hidden cove.

"They're here," Chaya murmured through clenched teeth. "There goes our chance for the boat. George is with them."

"You recognize his voice?"

She nodded.

"We need to get closer so we can see how many and maybe overhear what they're planning," Josh said.

Chaya cringed. "I've been close enough to last a lifetime."

"You wait here," Josh offered.

She swallowed. "What kind of princess would I be if I skipped out after you kissed me back?"

"That's my girl."

"I thought Elizabeth was your girl."

"Elizabeth doesn't know any interesting Sasquatches. Ready?"

She sighed again, then nodded, a quick careful bob of her head.

Chaya with her unloaded rifle and Josh in a martial artist's stance crept through the fog and drizzle toward voices now raised to a scolding level. Just this side of the near boulder, a deadfall of drift logs and brush formed a barrier from behind which they sneaked a peek into the cove.

They saw a small cabin cruiser tied up in the cove and three men ashore, their faces barely distinguishable in the mist. Nonetheless, Josh recognized the two Indians he had seen yesterday fleeing Chaya's Sasquatch impersonation. One was short and stocky with a big nose and black hair in a bowl-cut. The other was skinny with short hair. A *Patriots* baseball cap dripped water off its brim in front of his eyes. Both wore matching canary-yellow thigh-length slickers big enough to conceal handguns.

The third man was angrily ripping the Indians a new one. He was a white man over six feet tall with the jawbone of an ass and shoulders broad enough to force him to walk sidewise through most doors. A formidable-looking individual, he appeared to be about Josh's age, perhaps younger. He wore rubber boots and a military poncho. He could have easily snapped his wife's neck and made it look as if she had fallen. The question of why he hadn't done just that became clear in the tirade with which he blistered his henchmen.

"You incompetent pieces of— What the hell am I paying you for? You were supposed to have the job finished by the time I came back."

"You said she didn't have a gun," the Skinny Indian whined.

"I said she didn't have any *bullets*. Obviously, I was wrong, as that fool Dunelle found out. I hope you buried the bastard deep so he don't stink and the bears dig him up."

"The *dsonoqua* will kill us," Bowl-Cut complained.

The white man glared at him. "Sasquatch doesn't exist except in the minds of red fools."

"But…"

"Never mind. We have to finish the job now that it's started. Get it over with so I can run back to Bella Bella and establish another alibi before I come back and find the body. You'll get your money when I get mine."

Tears flooded Chaya's eyes. "George," she mouthed, identifying him. Josh squeezed her hand. This had to be hard on her, confirmation by his own mouth that the man she married was indeed behind the plot to murder her.

"She was in the cabin when it burned," Skinny Indian protested. "She could not have got out. There were two of them."

"*What?*" George turned on him. The Indian shrank away.

"I—I, uh, saw a man tied up in a chair when I fired the cabin."

"Why would she have a man tied up, you idiot?"

Bowl-Cut managed an uneasy joke. "So he'd stay with her and not run off?"

Josh thought George was going to jump on him and strangle him. Instead, he controlled himself and asked, "Did you find a boat?"

The Indians looked at each other.

"Then how the hell could he have got here? Did you find his body in the ashes?"

The Indians went sheepish.

"You haven't looked, have you? You two are bigger fools than Dunelle."

George raged back and forth in the rain slinging his arms in frustration and anger. The man had a temper. He suddenly pulled a pistol from underneath his poncho and thrust it to within two inches of Skinny's nose, right beneath the bill of his *Patriots* cap. His head lowered with crocodilian menace, eyes cold with cruelty as old as time. The prospect of easy money—and lots of it—did strange things to men.

"A bullet for your stupidity is what you deserve," he threatened. Skinny seemed about to wet his pants. Maybe he did. George lowered the gun after a tense second. "I won't kill you," he promised, "if you don't screw up anything else."

"No sir no sir no sir..."

George laughed without mirth.

"They can't have gone far in the dark even if they escaped the fire," he said. "I suppose I'll have to handle this myself. You stay here and guard the boat. Don't even think of doing anything stupid—like trying to run out on us. I'd hunt you to the ends of the earth."

Skinny obviously believed him. George twirled a ring of keys in his face.

"Besides, I have the boat keys."

He returned keys and pistol beneath his poncho. Bowl-Cut nervously patted a bulge beneath his slicker.

"She will not get away this time," he vowed.

"Shoot the man, if there *is* a man. Don't shoot her. It has to be an *accident*."

"She could maybe shoot herself by accident."

George withered Bowl-Cut with a look. He jabbed a forefinger into his chest. "Grab the rifle from the boat and come with me. That bitch's ashes *will* be found in the cabin."

Chapter Fifteen

George and Bowl-Cut left on the trail uphill toward the cabin. Fog swallowed them quickly. Left alone with only a spare rifle for company, Skinny appeared as nervous as a cat in a room full of mouse traps. He paced back and forth in front of the beached boat, starting at every sound, pausing every few steps to cock his head and listen, dark eyes scanning the forest as though expecting a werewolf to leap out of the mist.

"Bad timing that my bearskin burned," Chaya mused. "Another glimpse of Sasquatch and he'd learn to walk on water. But even if we get past him, we'd never get the boat started. George took the key."

"I grew up in Chicago," Josh whispered back.

She looked quizzical.

"You never heard of hotwiring a car?"

"I *didn't* grow up in Chicago."

"I guess juvenile delinquency finally pays off. *Shhh!*"

Skinny had keen hearing. He stared directly at the drift. Josh and Chaya waited with bated breath and thumping hearts. Finally, they heard the crunch of seashells and pebbles underneath boots as Skinny resumed his watch.

"Give me the rifle," Josh instructed, speaking in an even lower whisper than before. Barely mouthing the words.

"It's not loaded," she replied in the same manner.

"He won't know that—not after what you did to Dunelle."

"Oh, Josh. I didn't want to—"

"If we had another bullet, I'd shoot this one and not lose a wink of sleep. Not after what he tried to do to you."

Skinny reached the far apogee of his pattern. He started back. Josh shook his head to warn Chaya. She handed him her rifle. Rain still drizzled down off Skinny's bill cap in front of his face.

Skinny paused and looked about uneasily. It wasn't Sasquatch who was going to drive a stake through his heart.

Josh waited for the right moment. Skinny attempted to light a cigarette. It caught flame, but he tilted his ball cap the wrong way and spilled water off the dented crown, soaking the cigarette and putting it out. Skinny slammed it to the ground and issued a blistering line of swearing that he probably hadn't learned from his mother. He turned around to pace some more.

Josh went into action, his heart hammering so hard he was sure the Indian must surely hear it. He crabbed around the end of the drift logs and charged Skinny's rear. He was within a half-dozen steps of his target when the Indian heard him and pivoted about. Surprise flashed across his features. Josh covered him with Chaya's empty rifle, knowing he had better run the best poker bluff of his life.

"Go ahead, make my day," Josh snarled in his best imitation of Clint Eastwood as *Dirty Harry*.

The Indian's weapon hung at the end of his arm.

"You're not loaded," Skinny stammered, staring into the barrel pointed at his face.

Still in role, Josh growled, "You willing to bet your pathetic life on it, scumbag?"

Skinny wasn't.

"Drop the rifle," Josh ordered.

It fell to the beach with a clatter. Josh gestured with his weapon.

"Back up and assume the position."

The Indian stared. Apparently he didn't watch cop shows.

"That means lie face down on the ground."

The Indian did as directed, shifting his gaze from Josh and the rifle to Chaya when she came running up. She snatched up Skinny's discarded weapon and checked to make sure *it* was loaded. Satisfied, she trained it on its former owner. Josh let out a long breath of relief.

An opportunity like this presented itself once in a lifetime. He took a step toward the prone would-be killer and thrust the muzzle of his rifle against Skinny's head. He thought the Indian was going to wet his pants again. He squeezed the trigger. The metallic snap of the hammer striking an empty chamber—and Skinny *did* wet his pants. Dirty Harry would have been proud.

"You were right," Josh said. "It wasn't loaded."

Chapter Sixteen—

Hotwiring an engine, whether automobile or boat, couldn't be that difficult. Josh had seen it done in *The Night of the Living Dead.* Or was it in *I Saw What You Did Last Night.* The inference he made to Chaya about his juvenile delinquency was only so much bluster; if anything, he had belonged to the nerd herd. What he knew was theory—bypass the starter switch and make a direct connection between the battery and the starter.

The engine refused to make a sound. He shot a look to where Chaya held the Indian face down at gunpoint on the beach. The tide was coming in, nibbling at Skinny's boots. He withdrew his feet.

"Don't even think about it," Chaya warned. He believed her after Dunelle.

She seemed to have everything under control. Josh flipped the lid to the inboard and sprawled on the deck to poke around in the engine. Cold rain pecked at his back. He soon discovered what appeared to be the problem. The distributor cap was missing. George obviously hadn't trusted Skinny not to haul out on him, so he had taken a little extra precaution. The Kris Kraft was going nowhere except to rise with the tide.

They had been this close, *this close*, to escaping.

"The bastard took the wiring," he called out to Chaya.

"It won't start?" she cried, alarmed.

"Not without divine intervention."

Frustrated and with renewed dread at the prospect of being trapped on the peninsula with a gang of felons led by the lady's husband, not to mention the marauding grizzly, Josh dashed into the boat's tiny cabin to scrounge around in hopes George may have hidden the engine part aboard.

He was bent over going through a box full of oily spare parts when he heard a low muffled scream, followed by the rapid crunching and shuffling of boots. He snapped erect and saw through the windscreen the rain—and fog-shrouded forms of three men. It was clear what had happened. George and Bowl-Cut had slunk back under cover of the mist and surprised Chaya before she had time to utter a warning. George had Chaya in a headlock, bent back in a painful and awkward position that almost cut off her breathing. In the other hand was a pistol pointed at the boat.

Skinny back on his feet had reclaimed his rifle from Chaya. He and Bowl-Cut were advancing toward the boat, cautious but nonetheless confident. By this time they knew their prey was unarmed.

So much for the *Dirty Harry* act.

Josh's options seemed limited. Being captured meant his and Chaya's death warrants were sealed, in the dialogue of the old TCM Cagney movies. That left one option, considering he was one man with a sheath knife against three whose weapons *were* loaded.

Run!

Fortunately, the boat windows were fogged-up. The hardcases ashore failed to detect him until he dived through the hatch onto the aft deck. A rifle shot cracked hard and spiteful, shattering glass.

"You damned fool!" George shouted. "You shot the boat."

Josh plunged over the transom and landed in water up to his thighs, with the boat between him and the shooters. He splashed ashore, reaching dry land a desperate moment ahead of Bowl-Cut and Skinny, who came charging around the boat's high prow shouting at each other and being shouted at by George.

The Chicago Way was to get going when trouble broke out. Josh plunged headlong for the forest, running harder than he had since bullies tried to hijack him for his lunch money on the way to school. Two more shots pounded the fog, adding impetus to his impetus. One bullet barely missed. It gouged into a pine tree and stung his face with flying bark.

Then he was among the dripping trees. Behind him, the two Indians, Chaya's Jack the Ripper husband and Chaya disappeared in the mist. She was putting up a fight. Josh heard George shout a painful curse as she kicked him, head-butted him… Something. He hoped she got him where it hurt most.

"That'll be your last miserable time, slut," George howled. "Who the hell was that you're sleeping with when I'm gone?"

He sounded indignant at the thought that his wife might have a lover, never mind that he plotted to murder her.

Josh was off the trail. He knew he sounded like the stampeding iguana-monster in *The Land That Time Forgot* as he crashed through underbrush. It couldn't be helped.

He heard George bellowing through the mist. "Don't just stand there, you idiots? Catch him and kill him. I'll take care of the bitch—and I'll enjoy every flaming minute of it."

Chapter Seventeen

The giant prehistoric crocodile in *Croc* had chased the girl wearing the teeny-weeny itsy-bitsy polka dot bikini through the woods. She ran for her life; everyone knew she couldn't escape. Josh seemed to be in the same predicament now. Foremost in his mind, however, was not fear for himself as much as it was fear for Chaya. Guilt also. Guilt that he had deserted her.

Guilt at discovering that, in teaming with Chaya, he was more-or-less abandoning Elizabeth. Guilt was a tireless horse.

There was something about Chaya and her indefatigable courage, the haunting sadness in her green eyes when she accepted the truth that her own husband was going to kill her for the insurance, the scent of her hair and her breath when they lay face to face last night in the tent with only the fabric of the sleeping bag separating them, the brief sweet taste of her lips on his...

Nobody believed in love at first sight anymore. That was so yesterday, so *Hallmark Channel*. Today, it was hook up, unhook, and be on your way to the next tryst. Still, what Chaya and he had shared together in less than twenty four hours was more than Elizabeth and he had shared in a year.

His fear turned to seething anger. He couldn't turn her loose like this after only having just found her in a Sasquatch suit.

Fog and drizzling mist in the forest closed around him like a clammy glove. He was forced to break trail for his pursuers, stumbling over felled trees, crawling through brush on all fours, sometimes bouncing off tree trunks before he saw them. His breath felt harsh and raw in his throat. His heart hammered in his chest.

The Indians were gaining on him, following his clearly-marked trail. He circled wide and uphill back toward the cabin. His mind raced to come up with a workable plan of action. One would have thought he could devise something after all the old Saturday Night horror movies he had watched with Elizabeth. In the films, it seemed the hero and heroine always destroyed the thereat with fire, flood, dynamite or a nuclear explosion. In *The Bone Eater*, Bruce Boxleiter donned war paint and a buckskin jacket and, armed with a sacred bone tomahawk, confronted the monster *mano a mano*.

Josh possessed no sacred tomahawk. Neither was he likely to find fire, flood, dynamite or a nuclear bomb.

From the way George talked, Josh knew he was dragging his wife to the ashes of the cabin, there to burn her to death in order that her body might be found in the "accidental" fire. Josh had no idea what he was going to do even if he reached Chaya and her murderous husband in time. All he knew was that he had to reach her. Desperation seemed to lend wings to his feet. If only he had real wings and could spit fire like the creatures did in *Gargoyle*.

The timber thinned somewhat, although with the fog he could still see no more than a few feet in any direction. He thought he might soon intersect the trail where he had taken his nap and first encountered Chaya as Sasquatch. That trail, if he could find it, led to the clearing, the burnt cabin and, hopefully, Chaya.

He expected his pursuers to heave into view out of the mist at any time, rifles blazing to cut him down.

"You might as well pack it in, mate!" one of the Indians shouted. Probably Bowl-Cut. "Save us all a bundle of trouble."

"You can't get away," Skinny chimed in. "You and your girlfriend are bait for bears."

Rain blurred Josh's vision. He kept swatting at his eyes to clear them. He blinked and suddenly broke free of the trees onto a trail. He hesitated, unsure if it was the right path, head snapping in either direction to decide which way he should go. He was almost certain the cabin lay to the right, but he took a last look to the left to reinforce his decision.

An enormous dark form, erect on hind legs, passed in and out through the fog, visible only for the blink of an eye, into view and out again. A scene from a horror flick. It had to be the grizzly, but he couldn't be sure.

He turned in the opposite direction, to the right, and plunged recklessly towards where he hoped to find the cabin. As Satchel Page so famously said, "Never look back. You never know what might be gaining on you."

Josh heard the Indians baying in triumph as they came upon the trail. Now, it became a footrace. None of the bookies in Chicago would have taken bets on the outcome.

"This way," Bowl-Cut yelled to Skinny.

Skinny's response was cut short by a scream of such utter terror that it seemed to erupt from the dark bowels of the earth. A low, deep growl followed. More horrendous screams. Sounds of a violent struggle, a gunshot. Then—silence as deep as the fog.

Josh didn't look back.

Chapter Eighteen

The thing Josh saw through the mist didn't *look* like a bear. *Whatever* it was saved his butt and gave him a fighting chance at reaching Chaya in time. If George heard the shot and the screams, he would undoubtedly assume it to be Josh's big death scene.

Although out of wind, desperation and determination lent him the strength and will to continue. The trail cut to the north and back east. At a bend in the trail, he recognized the log where he had napped and knew he was heading in the right direction. He sped up his pace.

It wasn't much of a run after that to the edge of the clearing. He stopped in the trees to study the charred ruins of the cabin. Everything lay in silence, both ahead at the ashes and behind him where the Indians were *detained*.

He caught movement in the mist and recognized George's massive bulk. Chaya lay crumpled at his feet, either unconscious or, worse yet, dead on the fire-blackened grass near where the cabin's front door had been. The seared door frame remained standing but askew; rafters and wall logs had collapsed and were mostly burned. Tendrils of smoke rose from hot spots.

Josh's heart sank. He was too late.

George looked about suspiciously. Josh shrank into the shadows. Satisfied, George returned to the business at hand. He dragged Chaya's body through the door frame into what had previously been the living room/kitchen. He returned for the gasoline container he must have brought from the boat. While Josh watched in horror, still trying to think of a plan, George drenched Chaya with gasoline. Acrid fumes even from across the clearing watered Josh's eyes.

Anger seared his soul and replaced clear vision with a red film. Whether she was dead or still breathing, he couldn't permit this outrage. Had he had time for analysis, he would never have believed himself capable of killing another human being. But this was a time only for action.

His entire being focused with an emotion akin to hatred upon the man who produced a cigarette lighter from underneath his rain-slick poncho. He flicked a flame and tented a hand above it against the drizzle. George's rifle was leaning against the door frame outside his reach.

Josh succumbed to his rage with a roar unlike anything he had ever produced before, unlike anything he had ever heard. George was bending over to touch fire to his wife when the sound grabbed him by the throat and twisted him about. Surprise flashed huge across his face. A gust of rain wind extinguished the flame in his fist.

Even as Josh charged across the clearing, he noticed movement in the cabin ruins. Chaya sat up suddenly, shedding wet ashes. She saw Josh and cried out at the unbelievable sight of a man who, a stranger not so long ago, was willing to risk his life to save hers.

Tears of disbelief blurred Josh's vision. *She lived!*

Hitting George was like running into *The Incredible Hulk*. Josh bounced off, almost losing his footing. George waded in immediately and would have promptly finished him off with a flurry of blows had he not been hampered by the billowing poncho he wore. Josh attempted to respond, getting in one or two fast hard jobs directly into the big man's face. Blood spurted, but George didn't so much as blink as he pressed the fight.

Josh threw himself between the big man's hammering arms and attempted to grapple him to the ground. Although game, he was no match for a man stronger and more vicious than anything Josh had ever confronted in Chicago.

George pushed him off and caught him with a sharp hook to the jaw. While Josh was reeling from that one, a straight right sent him crashing to the mat. Before he lost consciousness, he saw Chaya crawling toward her husband's rifle. George turned and snatched it from her hands.

"I'll finish off the two of you myself, I will," he roared.

Oblivion descended upon Josh's world, preceded by something dark, huge and fierce storming out of the woods on two legs.

Chapter Nineteen

Chaya was helping him to his feet. He was still groggy from George's punches, still in both this world and the next from which he never expected to return.

"Wha... Wha...?" he stammered.

"He's gone," Chaya said.

Josh focused his eyes and his hearing. He slowly looked around, still in a daze. There was no sign of

George, other than his rifle discarded in the clearing halfway between the cabin and the forest. The fog was lifting, the rain easing. A shaft of golden sunshine rayed through the clouds.

"G-Gone?"

He stood unsteadily on his own feet, weaving slightly. Chaya wouldn't let him go. It was like she couldn't get close enough.

"I—I saw George with the rifle. He—I thought you were... I thought we were both dead."

"Sasquatch saved us."

It took a moment for something like that to sink in. Was she crazy? Were they both mad? He recalled as from an old dream the last thing he remembered seeing before he passed out—the upright hairy giant on the periphery of his vision, charging at George from the forest. The same apparition he had witnessed seconds before Skinny and Bowl-Cut encountered something terrifying on the trail, from which they apparently had not survived.

None of it made sense. He was not living a horror movie—*Pterodactyl* or *Vampire Slayer*. This was *real life*. Things like a Sasquatch didn't happen in *real life*, did they?

"It's bad luck to see a Sasquatch," was the only thing he could think to say.

"For *them*," she said, overcome with joy.

Chaya clutched him so tightly he couldn't breathe. He turned in her arms. She tilted her head and pulled his down to hers. Their lips met in a long, sweet kiss that blotted out everything except the kiss. Plenty of time later to sort it all out. At the moment, his only thought was that he was no longer lost.

Warm Love on Cold Streets
Jackie King

Jackie King loves books, words, and writing tall tales. She especially enjoys murdering the people she dislikes on paper. She has published four *Foxy Hens* novellas; a traditional mystery, *The Inconvenient Corpse*; a nonfiction book, *Devoted to Cooking*; and dozens of short stories about women. She lives in Tulsa, Oklahoma in a comfortable clutter of books and papers.

For my sister
Joan Sprague McNeely

Prologue

The trick was to wear black and to stand so still you disappeared into the night. Movement attracted attention. Become one with the darkness and move like a panther. Tulsa must be cleansed of human filth—one piece of garbage at a time.

The streets hadn't always been filled with dregs of society. Mother said there were no homeless on the streets back in the sixties. Downtown was a place for decent folk. Women dressed up in high heels and white gloves, sometimes even hats. They made special trips downtown with their lady friends to spend the day shopping and to have a nice lunch. Dirty men didn't wander around asking for handouts or huddling in alleys with a cheap bottle of booze. Or getting high on drugs.

Nowadays, women did some night crawling, too. *Women*! Women with no pride or decency left in them. But the men were the worst. The men must be eliminated first, and then the women. A person couldn't think about how many needed to die. The job would seem overwhelming. Clear away one piece of trash at a time, just like Mother showed me all those years ago, when the neighborhood was overrun with feral cats.

"You can't let yourself feel bad about killing these filthy creatures," Mother had said, "you must be strong—like I'm strong."

Then she'd handed me a chocolate mint patty to eat, so I wouldn't cry. She even let me put a candy on kitty's head, and that made me feel better. Now I'm grown up and strong like Mother was then. I no longer feel bad about doing what is necessary... but I still leave the mint.

Tonight the garbage had sheltered inside a large cardboard box with his booze. He thought he was safe, nestled between a Dumpster and a snow drift. Ragged and filthy—stinking of cheap alcohol and urine and vomit—this one couldn't be allowed to draw breath for another night. Nature's mistakes must be corrected, tidied up. Like an unmade bed in a fine hotel. I'll remove one useless person after another until Green Country is once again wholesome and fresh smelling.

A quick pull removed the cork from the tip of an old fashioned ice pick. Was the slight squeak imagined or real? It was hard to know. The chipped wooden handle felt familiar and comfortable; a feeling of power surged like an electrical current. One soundless thrust through a closed eye brought success. And sensual relief.

Chapter One

"This makes four dead." Detective Mike Morgan hunched his shoulders against the cold and blew on his fingers to warm them. Why had he forgotten his gloves? "That's one murder a week since Christmas Eve."

"Yup, it's the same MO," his partner Joaquin Sanchez agreed. "And he's left that damned chocolate mint on the guy's forehead again. The media will have a field day if they get hold of that detail."

"You're right. Let's hope that no one leaks that to the press." Mike stepped back and motioned the CSI member forward.

"The Captain said if there was another killing, one of us would have to go undercover," Sanchez said.

"Then I guess I'd better skip shaving tonight. There's no use in you not being home with your kids." Mike stamped his feet to warm them. Why couldn't this have happened in the spring instead of the worst winter in history?

"What kind of a meal can I make with wonton wrappers and fortune cookies?" Anna Rainwater kept her voice low so her kitchen trainees wouldn't hear. "I can't spin gold out of straw!"

"Sure you can. You did it yesterday. And the day before." Rosie Watkins, her best friend and fellow employee, also spoke just above a whisper. "Well, maybe not gold, but these folks aren't fussy. Brass will be fine—or even plastic for that matter." She nodded toward the three food trainees chopping vegetables at a large stainless steel worktable in the center of the kitchen, just on the other side of the storage area where they were talking. "That bunch of guys thinks you can work a miracle. That's what gives them the hope that you'll help them find a decent job."

Then God help them, Anna thought. She had her MBA and was cooking in a downtown mission. Eighteen months earlier she'd been vice president of a local company and gourmet cooking had been her hobby. Now she was trying to figure out how to feed 75 homeless men and women with stuff not even listed in the food pyramid.

Damned rotten economy! What was she supposed to do with three cases of wonton wrappers and two cases of fortune cookies? And why, in a moment of insanity, had she volunteered to train homeless men as sous chefs?

The back door slammed and Rex Martin, owner of an independent grocery store, carried in another armload of scrounged-up supplies. Gladys Ferguson, his long-time fiancée, trailed close behind. It amused

Anna that Gladys wouldn't let Rex out of her sight. Especially if another woman was anywhere near.

Rex, born and raised in Tulsa, had connections with many supermarkets, restaurants, and bakeries in the area. The man was a godsend and usually so was his assorted collection of donated foodstuff. But it had snowed every day since Christmas Eve and the sun seemed to have disappeared forever. Anna was a sunshine girl and the gloomy weather threatened to turn her even temperament into that of the Wicked Witch of the West.

"This is the last of it today," Rex said with a cheery smile. "I'm not sure what you can make with all of this, but we just take whatever is offered."

"If you don't want it, we'll take it up the road to John 3:16," Gladys said in her usual acid tone.

"Now, Gladys," Rex said.

"We appreciate whatever we get," Anna answered calmly, refusing to be offended. "You're really good to come each day with whatever is available."

"And now we have to get back to a *paying* job." Gladys whirled on her heel and stalked out of the room.

"That Gladys," Rex said sheepishly. "She's real high strung."

"No need to apologize. We're glad for your help." Anna watched him turn and follow Gladys out the back door.

"Poor henpecked guy," Rosie said. "Why do you suppose he puts up with that?"

"Same reason he excuses her bad manners as 'high strung.' He doesn't like confrontation with someone tougher than him. And who can blame him?" Anna said with a smile. She cocked her head to one side and perused the boxes of foodstuff. "And now, what to cook for lunch?" She thought for a moment, then a slow smile curled her lips. "Oh, yeah. That should work."

"Woo hoo!" Rosie laughed. "I can see the wheels turning in that brain of yours. We're gonna be eating good."

Mid afternoon Rosie bundled up in her winter gear and stepped outside for a cigarette. Anna followed soon after. The alley was one of the few places they could talk privately. Anna wondered how many soup kitchens had their managerial meetings in an alley, then smiled. When Luther went to St. John's for surgery and long-term rehab, the women hadn't changed their earlier habits. No need to. No one cared how they ran the place—just so the homeless got fed.

"I must really love you to risk both lung cancer and pneumonia for our chats." Anna pulled her heavy wool muffler over her mouth and nose for protection against the bitter wind and to help screen the headache-provoking smoke.

"I'm going to quit real soon," Rosie said as she always did. "Just as soon as things level out with my grandkids and I get a better job."

"Yeah," Anna said with a grin. "That's the same time I'm going to find my prince charming and settle down happily ever after."

Rosie snorted. "Yeah, girlfriend, we got our futures mapped out perfectly. By the way, that was some kick-assed soup you conjured up for lunch. Who'd ever thought of using wonton wrappers in regular Okie soup? What'd you do, grind up some chicken to tuck inside those little thing-a-ma-bobbies?"

"Chicken vegetable dumpling soup, my latest gourmet-on-the-cheap recipe. Wait until you try the apple crunch at supper. I've got the guys crushing fortune cookies to use as crust and topping."

"That's my girl. The gold-from-straw spinner."

"Sorry I've been cranky lately. I'm grateful you found me this job. It sure beats nothing, and at least it's not dull." Anna sighed. "Not that there's anything wrong with dull. Dull is okay. Dull typically doesn't include misery, and that's good." Anna shivered.

"Why you shivering like a goose just stepped on your grave?" Rosie asked.

"Because it's freezing?"

"That's no ordinary shiver. That's your hounds-of-hell-are-after-us shiver. I've seen that shiver before and I don't like it one bit."

The hounds-of-hell-are-after-us shiver. That was pretty accurate. Rosie knew her too well. Anna had also recognized the shiver—but she didn't intend to either explain it or defend it. She couldn't, because she didn't understand it herself.

"Oh crap," Rosie said, her plump, mahogany-colored face twisting into a scowl. "You got those heebie-jeebies again. Last time I saw that shiver Dr. McDreamy was about to bail on you."

The words jarred Anna, and it was a minute before she could speak. She'd never told Rosie how much she hated her best friend naming her fiancé after the star of Grey's Anatomy.

"I got to go inside, I've taken a long enough break." She turned on her heel and crunched through the snow to the back door.

"Oh crap," Rosie breathed under her breath.

Anna stepped into the back storage room and closed her eyes to collect her thoughts. The painful lurch in her heart at the mention of Kevin Baldwin, Rosie's "Dr. McDreamy," had left her unnerved. She so wanted to be over him. It wasn't just that she had loved him; the problem was that she had *trusted* him. Completely. For 20 years. Theirs was supposed to have been a bond so strong that marriage vows were superfluous. At least that was what Kevin had claimed all those years earlier.

After he had gone, her analytical mind had recognized his selfishness. He had used her to accomplish his own goals but he had never meant to grow old with her. She'd put him through medical school and residency and the years needed to establish his successful practice. When Anna's youth changed into the patina of maturity, he forgot his promises, and had proposed marriage to a younger woman born into money.

The door opened and a burst of cold air chilled Anna's back. The odd mingling of jasmine cologne and nicotine assailed Anna's nose and was followed by warm arms circling her waist.

"Me and my big mouth," Rosie said. "What do I know about shivers? Maybe you're just reverse-flashing."

"Maybe so," Anna agreed, enjoying the comfort of her friend's embrace. A second shiver ran down Anna's spine but she closed bad thoughts out of her mind. "Menopausal miseries—that's what it is—and too many cloudy skies."

She and Rosie had forged an unlikely friendship the minute they met 15 years earlier. At that time Anna was manager of finance for an engineering firm and had hired Rosie as her file clerk. The CEO questioned her about choosing a woman of fifty with no office experience when there were younger applicants with technical skills. Anna explained that the choice would look good on their government quotas for minorities.

That had been less than the truth. Anna had recognized the innate intelligence in Rosie's dark eyes. And something else. She'd seen the haunted look of a woman trying to get a clerical job with benefits, so she could ditch her fast food preparation job. Rosie was raising two grandchildren and desperately needed medical insurance for her family.

An intangible bond had formed almost immediately—unlikely, inexplicable, permanent. When

Anna was promoted to vice president, she made Rosie her personal assistant. She never regretted the choice.

Both had been laid off on the same day by the male dominated company, and neither had been able to find a comparable job. "Over qualified," they had been told. The two women had been out of work almost two years when Rosie called and said she had found jobs for them. That was seven months earlier. Anna was desperate enough to consider anything.

"Two jobs are available at *Luther's Haven*. One is for a cook and the other is for a general clerk—meaning 'gofer,' I think. You're a great cook and I'm a great 'gofer'," Rosie said over the phone. "We're perfect for the jobs. There's only one little drawback."

Anna had paused for a second. "Two questions. What sort of bar is *Luther's Haven* and what's the *little* drawback?"

"It's not a bar, honey, it's a soup kitchen—a day mission—where they feed homeless folks. I'd think a bleeding heart liberal like you would leap at the chance to cook for the downtrodden. They'll probably be a hell of a lot more appreciative than that bunch of executives and their wives you used to entertain with your fancy cooking."

"I entertained because I love to cook. I never had any illusions." But she had. She'd thought the other executives had accepted her as one of them. When the CEO called her in and gave her walking papers, she'd been completely blindsided.

"Sure you loved entertaining," Rosie said. "But you also thought those folks were your friends. I know your feelings were hurt when you lost your job. That bunch kicked your ass so hard that you're *still* walking funny."

It was time to change the subject. "So what's the *small* problem?" Anna asked.

"The mission is downtown, but there's a place where we can park in the back. No fee to pay. That's a huge plus, you know."

"Downtown? You know that I panic when I have to go downtown, especially at night. I was robbed once—held up by a jerk with a gun—just a block from the Brady Theater. Scared the crap out of me. I never go downtown alone at night. Never."

"Now don't freak out on me. Downtown has been cleaned up. It's as safe as a children's nursery."

"My cousin raised children," Anna said. "Ask her about the safety of a nursery. Ask any working mother. Those places are pestilence factories. Her kids contracted everything from head lice to mononucleosis at those nurseries."

"Oh come on. You'll be working mostly in the daytime. Only in the winter will you be driving home in the dark."

Anna's wool-gathering was interrupted by Rosie waving a hand in front of her face. "Where you gone to in that head of yours? You're daydreaming again. I see your eyes glazing over."

"Guilty as charged." Anna laughed, slipping off her puffy quilted coat. "And we both need to get back to work."

A third shiver slid through her, like an icicle down her back.

Rosie's eyes widened. "Hot flash!" she said. "Definitely a hot flash!"

Anna reached for Rosie's hand and squeezed it. A woman friend could be a formidable ally. The shrewd and practical-minded Rosie had no problem insisting that a hot flash could cause a shiver. And if necessary she would swear to it in a court of law with her hand on the Bible.

Chapter Two

No one wanted to eat slop on a plate, so Anna tried to make each meal pretty as well as tasty. She added a garnish of parsley to the plate she was filling and handed it to the next man waiting in line, along with her usual smile.

He looked into her eyes and Anna caught her breath, feeling as if she might drown in the blue of his eyes. He totally captured her gaze and for an instant she couldn't breathe. It was as if his Pacific blue eyes mesmerized her, turning her smile into a silly grin. He had light brown hair tied back in a ponytail, a square jaw and a nose that was a bit crooked—as if it had once been broken. But it was his eyes that turned her knees weak, as if she were a teenager and he a rock star. She forced herself to break eye contract, but she was shaken. Who was this fellow and what was wrong with her? If a homeless guy was turning her on, she was just plain pathetic.

Anna kept serving food by rote but her mind was on Blue Eyes. The man was new to the mission. This guy she would have remembered. Tulsa's reputation as a city with a heart had drawn many new homeless men and women to town. Word had traveled countrywide on an invisible pipeline and their clientele grew daily.

She scanned the room and saw the guy sit down at a front table with his back toward her. Her head cleared and her senses returned. What on earth was wrong with her? He was just another homeless man needing a good meal. She needed to get out more.

His coat looked warm and she was glad of that, and he wore a knit cap. She didn't see any gloves, but they could be in his pocket. She'd ask Rosie to find out if he needed a pair. There was a donation closet next to the food storage room.

* * *

Mike had deliberately faced the front window so he could study anyone who entered. He'd already perused those present and each had the unmistakable aura of homelessness. That haunted look and defensive body language were almost impossible to fake. His cover story was that he had recently been evicted from his house, then lost his car because of months of unemployment.

His thoughts roamed back to the brunette. He already knew that she was called Anna Rainwater, but he hadn't expected her to be so hot. She was a paid cook and not a do-gooder and she seemed out of place. Too classy. He finished his meal and carried his plate and plasticware to the trash container, then reseated himself at an angle so he could watch everyone in the room without seeming to. A cop's trick.

He'd been briefed about everyone working at the mission. Luther, the guy who had started the soup kitchen, was hospitalized for amputation of both his feet due to diabetes. He was currently in Kaiser Rehabilitation Center and was managing his employees by phone. The downturn in economy seemed to have provided him with better employees than were usually available. Mike was pretty sure that under normal circumstance the brunette wouldn't have considered working here.

The three men cleaning the kitchen were food prep trainees. They seemed eager to work toward a better life. The one called Curly was balding, and judging by how loud he spoke, was perhaps hard of hearing.

"I think I'll take a look at this morning's paper and see if there are any jobs available for cooks and such." Curly walked into the dining area and gathered up different sections of the paper scattered about. "Hey, there was another murder last night. The guy was stabbed in the eye with an ice pick while he slept." Curly read silently for a minute then shouted, "Oh crap, listen to this, the murderer left a chocolate mint on the dude's forehead."

A shocked silence fell over the group. These people were scared enough before, Mike thought, and now these lurid details had them terrified. And they had nowhere to hide. He sipped coffee gone cold and studied the room. When the news about the mint had been leaked to the media, he'd been sent undercover. This sort of grotesque detail made public had caused the mayor to start calling the chief and demanding answers.

"Crap, Curly, what else does it say?" someone said.

"The guy was offed just a couple of blocks from here." He turned to Anna who was still behind the counter. "What do you think about all of this, Annie? You scared when you leave at night? You have to walk to your car, don't you?"

"They're killing us homeless guys, dummy," another man shouted. "Anna will be all right."

"Everybody in this part of downtown is scared, Curly." Anna bit her lip. "Does the paper give the victim's name?"

"Naw, he most likely wouldn't have had identification. We knew most of the other murdered guys, though. I recognized them from their pictures in the paper." Curly wadded the paper and threw it into the trash.

Mike heard chairs being pushed away from the table and saw the crowd start to leave.

"What's wrong with you guys? Did I scare you all away?" Curly asked with a nervous laugh.

"Don't push it, Curly," Anna said. "No one wants to talk about the murders."

Mike decided he'd like to know Anna better and wondered if she'd be interested in going out with a cop. He hadn't dated for awhile and was missing a woman's company. The problem with dating was that it led to complications in his life. His longest relationship had been his former fiancée, Myrna Jones. The snazzy-looking blonde had siphoned away all of his savings, buying designer clothes and jewelry. The clerks at Miss Jackson's in Utica Square were on a first name basis with her. Myrna had been hot in bed and he'd been desperate to keep her. But when his savings were gone, so was Myrna.

He'd loved to watch Myrna talk. She didn't say anything of interest but her lips looked like Angelina Jolie's. Whether natural or not, he neither knew nor cared. He just loved to watch her pucker those luscious lips into a delightful, sexy pout that made him want to give her anything she wanted just to keep her in his bed. Maybe what he'd felt wasn't love, but he figured it was as much as he deserved. Cops made lousy boyfriends and worse husbands. He knew that because his father had been a policeman.

This woman's lips were thinner, more natural looking, nicely shaped, but in a more ordinary way. He watched her lick them now, as if they'd gone dry because she was scared. He decided it might be interesting to kiss her sometime after this case was settled.

Chapter Three

Seven days later the temperature was still below freezing and light snow fell sporadically. Anna donned her insulated coat and her wool cap and stepped outside. She propped open the mission's back door with a large rock kept nearby, then waved at the couple who were unloading boxes from the white Econoline van.

"Hey, there you two. I sure am glad to see that load of bread. I don't know what we'd do without you guys to cruise the bakeries and pick up their day-old stuff."

"We've also got produce and a bunch of frozen chickens," Rex said with a smile.

"Backs and necks," Gladys said.

"Bony pieces are great," Anna replied. "We'll make chicken enchiladas with that case of tortillas you brought a couple of days ago."

"I don't turn anything down," Rex said. "Not even the produce too wilted to sell."

"Those veggies work great in soup or casseroles," Anna said. Luther's was a privately run charity, and because of the recent economic downturn, donations had dropped. She smiled at Gladys Ferguson who scowled back. The woman was vinegary, but she always helped fetch and carry. If grumbling made her happy then Anna could endure that with a smile. "The two of you are a great help to this mission."

"We're glad to pitch in. By the way, how is Luther getting along?" A smile crossed Rex's face. "I was sure worried about him being in the hospital, but you and Rosie are doing a fine job."

"I ran by to see him yesterday afternoon. He's making good progress." Anna heard the back door open and Curly rushed in with a grim look.

"There's been another murder," he said. "Elgin and Archer—behind a building. Another homeless guy got nailed with an ice pick. I saw the headline through the newspaper box."

"Yes, I know," Anna said. "I saw the paper, too. When is this carnage going to stop?"

"We heard about it on the radio," Gladys said. "Good riddance of bad rubbish, I say."

"Gladys!" Rex said.

"If someone starts killing people that they consider to be rubbish, then you and I may be next," Anna said before she thought.

"Speak for yourself," Gladys huffed. "I work and earn my living."

"Lots of people aren't working just now. You want them all killed because they can't get a job?" Anna snapped, then bit her tongue and struggled to regain her poise. There was no use in sparring with Gladys. How on earth could a gentle guy like Rex put up with such an attitude?

"Well at least the murderer has a sense of humor. The news guy said a chocolate mint was left on his forehead again. Like those left on your pillow at a fancy hotel," Gladys said.

A hollow sickness spread through Anna. What kind of madman was loose in Tulsa? She turned to Rex. "I wonder who he was. Sure hope he's not one of our guys, again."

"I don't know, but the one before turned out to be that fellow with the ginger-colored whiskers. The one the guys called Red Beard. It was him," said Curly.

Anna caught her breath. Red Beard had seemed particularly vulnerable and always sat in the farthest seat in a corner, hunched over his plate. He talked to himself in a mumble, kept his gaze down and left as soon as he'd eaten. Medication might have helped, but most of the mentally ill wouldn't take pills. Were the men who came to their kitchen being targeted? Fear ran down her spine.

The first murder had occurred five weeks earlier on Christmas Eve, then continued with one more killed each week, like clockwork, on a Tuesday. Anna steeled herself and marched into the kitchen. She found a copy of the *Tulsa World* on one of the tables. "Chocolate Mint Killer Strikes Again," blazed across the front page. Anna shivered as she read the story. A year ago she had hesitated even driving in this part of town. Now she worked here and drove home in the dark every night.

She remembered the hot July day she came downtown to apply for the cook's job. She'd found Luther in the middle of a mess—men standing in line waiting to eat and one man trying to handle the chaos. If there was anything she'd learned in the corporate world it was how to handle a crisis.

Anna stepped behind the counter, positioned herself beside Luther and said, "I'm your new cook." He'd looked surprised for a minute then grinned and nodded. Anna had been astonished at how easily she was suited to cooking for a crowd.

She applied the same skills that had served her well in managing corporate employees. Three of the men had wolfed down their meal and stood to leave. "Hey guys," she called. "I could use some help back here. It's a lot cooler inside. Wouldn't you rather serve food in an air-conditioned kitchen than stand in 102 degree heat?"

Thus began her food prep training program.

Mike Sanders couldn't take his eyes off the brunette. Interesting that she was such a good cook, her being an out of work executive and all. Damn but he'd always liked shapely dark-haired women. Green eyes were icing on the cake.

She glanced up as if she could feel his gaze. Their eyes met and his heart quickened. Damn. He saw color rise in her cheeks and caught his breath. She felt that too, he thought, his spirits rising. It was the second time she'd noticed him.

He gave himself a mental shake. What was he thinking? Didn't he have enough problems living undercover as a homeless guy? He could smell his own unwashed body and his beard itched. He hated undercover when it required him to be filthy. In spite of his effort he'd had little success getting the other homeless men to talk to him.

The woman stood at the steel worktable and directed her crew, showing them how to cut fresh vegetables in some kind of a fancy way. He wondered if working here put her in any kind of danger. The thought was unexpected and he didn't like it. This was no place for anyone with a killer on the loose. He suspected the men from Luther's Haven were being targeted, but he had no idea why.

She smiled at the fellow across from her, a scruffy guy with a silly grin who seemed to be on way too familiar terms with his boss, in Mike's opinion. Jealousy stabbed him even though he knew it was ridiculous.

I need to keep my mind on my work, he thought. It was time to meet Sanchez and exchange information. He pulled on his goose-down coat, the one the other woman who worked here had wanted to mend. He'd managed to put her off. He'd had enough trouble getting that rip to look natural when he'd made it with his pocket knife. He stepped outside into the brutal wind and looked down the street. Detective Sanchez was walking up the sidewalk toward him, right on time. Their plan was for Mike to be arrested for vagrancy so they could exchange information. He slouched forward and put out his hand. Panhandling could never be easy, not even for the real homeless guys.

"Hey there buddy, could you spare a few bucks?"

The detective stopped and scowled. "Soliciting is against the law." With a quick, practiced movement he pulled Mike's arm behind his back and cuffed him. "You're coming with me." Then he pushed Mike toward an unmarked car parked nearby.

"Let go of me! I ain't done nothin'," Mike yelled.

Anna watched from the front window of the mission. The policeman's arrest of a man down on his luck blew through her like a hot angry wind. Didn't this guy have some real criminals to arrest? Without thinking she ran outside. The wind cut through her sweatshirt, chilling her to the bone. She hunched her shoulders and hugged herself.

"Just a minute," she called. "There's no need to arrest this man, he's not a vagrant. He's one of my food prep crew here at Luther's. I'm the cook and he works for me."

"Then he shouldn't be panhandling." Sanchez pushed Mike forward.

"He was soliciting donations for the shelter," Anna snapped. "There's nothing wrong with collecting money for charity. I'll call the media if you don't release him right now. I'll tell them the police are harassing the homeless, when they should be finding a murderer." She couldn't believe that those words had come from her mouth.

Mike saw his partner shift from surprise to shock to resignation. He looked back at Mike. "Watch yourself, buddy," he said with a dark look.

Mike could have strangled this well meaning hottie. The woman had botched their plans. He was trying to find a killer and she could easily blow his cover. He stared at her and waited to see what she did next. Another blast of arctic wind hit them and she shivered.

"Let's get inside before we freeze." She pulled at the door but the icy wind fought her.

Mike's instinct was to help, but knew that would be out of character. He watched her brace her legs and pull harder, wrestling the door open so they could step inside.

"Whew," she said. "Now what am I going to do with you?" She glanced up and he met her questioning gaze with a leer, knowing that would piss her off. She narrowed her eyes and stared at him without blinking.

Shame punched Mike in his gut, making him feel helpless and small. He had expected her to yell at him, perhaps to threaten to call the policeman back. Instead she entered into a staring contest that would have challenged a 20-year veteran cop. The woman had class and he had no idea of how to act around a classy woman.

He had to stay in character. The homeless part required him to play a rude and disgusting jerk. That was one of the types being targeted by the killer. He knew what he had to do, but God in heaven, he hated doing it.

Mike blew his nose on his fingers and wiped them on his dirty jeans. Then he hacked up what phlegm he could, opened the front door and spit on the sidewalk. This should put her off, he thought. For sure he was disgusting himself.

Her face remained expressionless. She turned and walked into the kitchen area, motioning for him to follow. He'd expected her to throw him out on the street. Instead she grabbed a giant sized bottle of germ killer and handed it to him along with some industrial quality paper towels.

"Sanitize your hands thoroughly then start peeling potatoes. I'll be watching, so if you so much as touch your face I'll spread the word to the men who eat here, and let them decide if they like eating snot."

"Yes, ma'am." Mike's words came out all wrong and sounded flirtatious. His tone had been pure male reflex and he knew he'd screwed up. What was wrong with him? Was he determined to blow his cover? This was no time to try and impress a woman. Especially the type of woman who could make a man to think of marriage. Cops had no business being married. Especially this cop.

Chapter Four

Anna felt such a fool. What was wrong with her? She had no business interfering with the police. She knew nothing about this man. Why in God's name hadn't she just let him be arrested? What was she thinking when she sided against a policeman? She liked cops.

For sure she was going to get out more. Find some nice guy to date, maybe. Regain her perspective. This man was disgusting. He'd blown his nose on his fingers and spit on the street. God help her! When it came to the opposite sex, she sure could pick them.

When was she going to learn? Hadn't Dr. Kevin Baldwin taught her anything? The chemistry between them had been instant and powerful and she'd wasted her youth on the jerk.

"We don't need a paper to bind us together," her Dr. McDreamy had said when she had met him years before. He was in medical school and she had been a senior at the University of Oklahoma. He was charming and she had believed every word he said during their years together. Even later when she had wanted to think about a baby and he talked her out of that idea.

"We don't want to be tied down with a child," he'd said. "There's plenty of time for kids later."

She had swallowed her disappointment and accepted his decision. *They* also had decided that she'd work so he could finish his schooling and then specialize in plastic surgery.

"What better investment could you make?" he'd said, charming her with his infectious grin. "When I'm making enough money we can start our family and you won't even have to work if you don't want to."

She hadn't even questioned his sincerity. She was too crazy in love to argue. She didn't even protest when Kevin put their house in his name only. What did it matter? What was his was hers, wasn't it? They were like Goldie Hawn and Kurt Russell, Anna had told herself.

The combination of their salaries allowed them a luxurious lifestyle and Anna floated on cloud nine for a little over 15 years. Then everything changed. He grew quieter and stopped confiding in her. The only time he asked for her opinion was regarding his wardrobe. One afternoon he insisted she help him choose new underwear. He'd always been a boxer man, now he wanted skimpy jockey's.

"You got a hot date?" she'd teased, not seriously considering such a thing, just trying to be amusing, to make him laugh.

"Don't be stupid," he'd snapped back, surprising her. "I just want something different."

She'd had no idea then that the "something different," was a young blonde. So she'd kept making excuses for him. Kevin was just under a lot of pressure. His job involved life and death. Her job only involved sums of money. Denial was an easy path.

She took a month long business trip to London and when she returned Kevin said she had to move out of his house, that he'd met someone else. God, she'd been stupid.

It had taken years to recover from the pain and the shock and the outrage. She'd put all her eggs into one basket as MeeMaw would have said, then the person she trusted most had crushed those eggs under his heel.

In an attempt to rebuild her life, she'd thrown all of her angry energy into her job and had been well rewarded. Then her second love, that same job, bit her in the butt, via the recession.

At first she'd been sure she would find another executive position. Top men from other engineering firms were always suggesting that perhaps she might like to come to work for them. But the bottom had dropped out of the American economy and the job market dried up. Those offers were no longer open.

Gradually she had been forced to change her lifestyle from luxurious to austere. She sold her red Lexus and bought a red Honda Civic; moved out of her downtown loft and into a small rent house on the east side of town. She struggled to make ends meet on a fraction of her former salary. Luckily she was better at economizing than most people her age because she'd learned thrift from MeeMaw. But the last thing she needed in her life was some deadbeat guy to support.

Suddenly it occurred to Anna that she didn't even know this homeless man's name. She turned back to him. "What should I call you?" she asked, and then she blinked. He was turning off the hot water tap and there were real soap bubbles circling the drain.

Anna handed him a paper towel. He kept his eyes focused on the process of hand drying, and then squirted germ-killer into his palms.

"Gus," he said. "Just Gus."

He sure didn't look like a Gus. But names meant nothing. Parents stuck their kids with the most awful monikers. She'd once had a girlfriend named Waynoka Fred. Luckily, her friends saved her by calling her Freddy.

"Well, Gus, I need that box of potatoes sitting on the floor scrubbed clean and chopped into pieces."

"Got it." He hefted the box and poured vegetables into the commercial-sized sink. "Where's the knife you want me to use?" Finally he met her gaze.

Something visceral swept through Anna. The sudden jolt of longing was as real as if she'd touched a live electrical wire. She'd felt this chemistry years before with Kevin, but had thought herself too jaded to ever experience such a thing again.

Anna sighed. As if her life wasn't complicated enough, now she had to wrestle with her libido. She was 47 years old and trusting a man was for young women. She pulled open a drawer filled with kitchen utensils. "Your choice." She whirled toward the walk-in refrigerator and almost collided with Rosie. Her friend grabbed her arm and pulled her into the soundproof refrigerator, closing the door behind them.

"I saw you talking to that guy and, Hallelujah, girl, I think you just came back to life—at least below the equator. Now just remember, you don't need some kind of special commitment with a fellow in order to sleep with him. Relax and enjoy yourself for once. You've lived way too serious a life."

"You're ridiculous. What would your Baptist friends think if they heard you saying that? And how can you read so much into a conversation? We were talking about peeling potatoes, for goodness sake."

"Humph. Don't lie to me, I know you too well. And I was listening with my eyes, and they heard plenty."

"You're imagining things," Anna snapped, but Rosie just giggled and waved goodbye. Her friend's words were nonsense, but that didn't keep them from replaying in her mind like a pesky tune that wouldn't fade.

You don't have to commit to a man to sleep with him.

He's homeless! Anna shouted inside her head. No sane woman would consider sleeping with a homeless guy about whose history she knew nothing. He might be on drugs and sharing needles. He might have a wife and six kids. Had she lost her mind? Was she that desperate to get laid? Time to buy a vibrator, she thought.

MeeMaw was old school Presbyterian and had hated her living with Kevin without being married. "Our family doesn't do that sort of thing," she'd said. Her grandmother would turn over in her grave at the thought of her even considering sleeping with a street person about whom she knew nothing.

Anna rolled her eyes. She was insane. Absolutely bonkers.

The January cold was brutal. Mike wrapped three blankets around him then added a plastic drop cloth to hold in his body heat. He scanned the area he'd picked to spend the night. There were other homeless gathered there and he'd positioned himself so he could keep watch over as many as possible.

An Arctic wind sliced through him, barely broken by his bedding. It was too cold to sleep outside, but he had to be where the action might occur. His assignment was to hang with the hard-core homeless until they were used to his presence—until someone told him something that might help uncover the Chocolate Mint Killer. Something which the person himself might not know was important.

When he closed his eyes a vision of Anna Rainwater flashed through his mind. He hadn't been able to keep his eyes off her at the mission. She'd ditched her becoming red bandana and put an ugly thing over her dark hair. A hairnet like the hospital gave you before surgery, white and opaque and ugly. She'd looked good even in that.

She directed her crew in a cross between big sister and army sergeant. Did her green eyes disturb other guys as much as they bothered him?

He smiled in self mockery. Idiot. She wouldn't be interested in a street bum. She might not even consider a cop. The woman was classy. He'd learned from Rosie that she was half Irish and half Cherokee, and for sure she was all woman. He hunched his shoulders for warmth and set himself for a long, miserable night.

The next morning started well for Anna. Gus fit right in with her crew and scarcely looked her way. There had been no need to switch from her red bandana to the opaque hairnet. She smiled at herself. You flatter yourself, girl. You're the only one getting turned on.

A shout and a hard knock at the back door heralded Gladys and Rex's morning arrival with supplies. Anna opened the door and slipped forward to help with the unloading. Halfway through Gladys dropped a bombshell.

"You'd better send this new fella packing. He's nothing but trouble. Neither Rex or me like him."

"Aw, Gladys, you hadn't ought to interfere." Rex shifted his feet and blushed. "It's none of our business."

"That's not what you said earlier this morning," Gladys snapped and Rex looked as if he'd like to sink through the floor.

"I saw that man blow his nose on his fingers yesterday and then spit on the street. He shouldn't be working in the kitchen."

"I make sure he scrubs his hands thoroughly with soap and hot water before touching food. I keep a close eye on cleanliness with all my crew."

"Did you know that he watches you?" Rex asked with a worried look. "He's real sly at it, but he never takes his eyes off of you for long."

"She likes that," Gladys said. "I've seen her give him the fisheye right back."

"How dare you," Anna snapped, shocked that Gladys could read her so well.

"I know what I see! Lie if you want to, but I say you've got the hots for that homeless fella."

"That's not true, is it?" Rex looked at Anna with troubled eyes. "A woman like yourself wouldn't even look at the likes of him. Would you?"

"This is absolutely ridiculous," Anna said. "Quit talking nonsense and let's finish unloading the van."

"Whee who!" Gladys shouted with a nasty laugh. "You notice, Rex, that she didn't deny she wants him."

Chapter Five

The noon meal was over when Rex Martin phoned saying he was a couple of minutes away with a load of day old bread. It was an unexpected delivery and Anna was delighted. Not wanting to distract her crew from cleaning the kitchen, Anna pulled on her coat and stepped outside to help unload.

Fresh blowing snow stung her eyes just as the van pulled into the alley, and then unexpectedly zigzagged. A dog yelped in agony, brakes squealed and then car doors opened and slammed shut.

"I tried to miss him," Rex shouted, "he ran straight under my wheels. Let me see how bad he's hurt."

"Don't even think of picking up that mongrel!" Gladys yelled. "He's filthy and probably has mange."

Rex stopped in his tracks and looked helplessly toward Anna. "It wasn't my fault, I swerved to miss him but he changed direction."

The black and white dog whimpered and started dragging himself toward Anna. His hind leg looked crooked and was probably broken. Her heart melted with pity. The animal was skin and bones and looked as if he were starving.

"I'll get a box from the storeroom so we can carry him into the kitchen where there's a good light to check him over." Anna stepped toward the back door.

"Let Rex take him into the woods and shoot him," Gladys said. "Put him out of his misery. No one needs another stray dog."

Anna stiffened and blood heated her cheeks. "Don't touch that dog until I come back," she said. Pushing the door open she grabbed a sturdy cardboard box and padded it with rags kept for cleaning.

She squatted beside the dog and considered how best to get him into the box without getting bitten. The animal whimpered and looked at her with soulful brown eyes. Anna's heart ached for him.

"I know it hurts, puppy, but if you'll let me pick you up, I'll get you to the vet."

"And who's going to pay the vet bill?" Gladys snapped. "Not me. Not Rex. None of this was our fault."

Anna ignored the woman, her heart was captivated by the sight of the starved-looking animal imploring her with chocolate colored eyes. A pitiful whimper melted her heart. The dog thumped his tail against the asphalt and cocked his head to one side, making puppy noises in his throat. His trusting look finished her off. What the hell. She'd figure out how to pay the vet somehow.

"No one wants him," Gladys said again. "Let Rex handle the problem."

"I want him," Anna said. She slipped her arms under the dog as carefully as she could and lifted him into the box. How she'd pay the vet bill was a problem to worry about later. Maybe she could negotiate a special price with the doctor.

Mike sensed something was wrong. Anna had been gone too long. No one would lounge about in the alley in this freezing weather. He grabbed his coat then stepped into the storage area just in time to see her snag a box and rags. He followed her outside.

He watched Anna deal with Gladys and with the dog. Everything he saw made him like her better. He'd made more inquiries about her and knew she was single. He also knew that he should mind his own business. Instead he stepped forward.

"I'll carry the mutt to your car." He picked up the box.

"Hey, fella, what do you think you're doing?" Rex asked.

"Oh let them go," Gladys said. "Two studs and one bitch. They can make a threesome."

Mike stopped in his tracks. If a man had said such a thing he would have put down the pup and given the bastard a lesson in civility. But this was a woman.

"My car's the Honda. Would you put him in the back seat, please?" Anna said. And then in a lower voice, "Sorry about that remark."

"Why? You didn't make it." Mike climbed into the rear so he could steady the box as she drove.

"I think I saw a veterinarian on Eleventh Street," she said, steering the car east.

Mike's heart sank. If that was the clinic he thought it was, he'd met one of the vets a few months ago. She had attended a neighborhood watch meeting where he had been a speaker.

Anna was a skillful driver and had no trouble negotiating the frozen streets. When she turned into the clinic Mike pulled his cap over his forehead and prayed he wouldn't be recognized. He carried the box toward the entrance. Anna stepped ahead and held open the door for him, then walked to the desk.

Mike watched her demeanor change—her posture, the set of her shoulders, the expression on her face—she morphed from a mission cook into an executive.

"I have an injured stray dog, here," Anna said. The tone of her voice wasn't arrogant or demanding, but when she spoke the receptionist stood and took both of them, along with the dog, to an examination room and promised that the doctor would come as soon as possible.

Anna kept her hand on the puppy's head and made gentle noises in her throat. These sounds seemed to comfort the animal, but disturbed Mike. They were sounds a mother might use to calm an infant and he was instantly aware of the emptiness in his own life.

The dog's eyes were closed now and his breathing seemed shallow. He no longer whimpered. Common sense told Mike that the pup would be better off if it never awoke. But Anna wanted the dog to live and he hated for her heart to be broken.

The door swung open and sure enough, Dr. Wong strode in, introducing herself. She was just as Mike remembered, mid-forties, medium height, a pleasant face framed by straight black hair. Anna explained the stray had been struck by a car in back of the mission. The doctor nodded as if she'd heard such stories before. She examined the animal with skillful hands and the young dog whimpered twice.

Mike kept his head down and did his best to disappear in plain sight—an undercover trick he'd developed over the years. He knew he was taking a risk when he accompanied Anna. He had lived all his life in this town and was acquainted with too many people. He hoped again that the vet wouldn't make the connection.

Dr. Wong took special care over the dog's bones and skeletal structure. Finally she turned to them. "The dog has a broken leg and maybe internal injuries. I need to take x-rays and blood work, and see what surgery will be needed. The doctor looked past Anna and studied Mike. Her face lighted with recognition. "Hey, I know you."

He was busted, but Mike believed in the power of denial. "Nope, I just got into town. I've never been in Tulsa before."

Dr. Wong cocked her head to one side and studied him. "Humm. Well, they say we all have a doppelganger somewhere. Yours is a policeman. He gave our neighborhood a really good lecture on urban safety a while back."

Mike shrugged. He watched Anna's reaction with his peripheral vision. Her eyes narrowed for an instant and she turned to study him. He couldn't tell what she was thinking. If she figured out who he was and what he was doing, he'd be taken off the case. He held his breath and waited. Anna turned to Dr. Wong.

"How much will all of this cost? I work as a cook at a downtown mission and can't afford much in the way of extra bills. You ever do pro bono work?"

She stopped talking and waited. Mike recognized that she was a skilled negotiator. His respect grew. Too bad they hadn't met at a better time; who knew what might have happened.

The doctor studied Anna, seeming to size her up.

"I donate some of my work to charity. But with the recession I've been swamped with more requests than I can grant. What could you pay?"

Mike decided he'd phone back with his credit card number. He may have screwed up the investigation, but at least he could save the dog.

"I could pay 20 percent of your usual fee—that would help with the cost of your overhead."

"How about I give you a 20 percent *discount*?" the doctor countered with a smile, showing this wasn't the first time she'd been in this situation.

Anna met her smile and offered to pay 30 percent of the total bill. The doctor refused and Anna played, what looked to Mike, like her trump card.

"A friend of mine works at the *Tulsa World*, and I'll bet he would run an article about your generosity. It would be great publicity for your clinic."

"Publicity, huh?" Dr. Wong grinned. She glanced at Mike then back at Anna.

"That would bring you more goodwill than a paid advertisement." Anna smiled.

The vet laughed out loud. "Sure," she said. "Why not?"

"And could you carry the note on my 30 percent? I'd sure appreciate it," Anna said. "I promise to pay forty dollars twice a month."

Mike watched Anna start the car and shift into drive. Would she be suspicious about who he was? Ask him questions about Dr. Wong recognizing him? Or had his denial worked?

"I've got to stop by the QuikTrip and buy a paper." Anna glanced sideways at Mike. "I've got to find a staff 'friend' and convince that person to write a heart warming story about a stray dog." She grinned.

Mike couldn't help laughing. He liked this woman's spirit. He liked *her*. He hoped to hell she hadn't tumbled to the fact that he was an undercover cop.

Anna kept her face expressionless. This guy was a policeman! Dr. Wong had recognized him, and even though Gus had denied it, neither she nor the vet had been convinced. She should have suspected that Gus wasn't homeless from the start. Now the truth seemed so evident. He was suspicious-minded and hard and jaded, but he'd stepped forward when she needed help with the dog. In her mind that was something a cop would do—a good one, anyway. He must be undercover because of the murders. That nasty little scene with the spitting and nose-blowing was just part of his cover— and she had interfered.

He must be worried that she was going to ruin his cover, but she wouldn't. She'd keep silent and pretend to be dumb as a rock. She might even be able to help him. After all, she knew the homeless better than he did.

A happy little glow lighted up her heart. This guy had a job!

Chapter Six

Anna Rainwater deserved to die! She was a phony. She pretended to be a righteous woman, but she was a slut. That made her more disgusting than the homeless. She should know better. Now she lusted over a street bum that wasn't worth the powder it would take to blow him to hell. There was no doubt about that. It made a person want to vomit. Maybe she'd always been trolling for men. She often moved from man to man at the mission, smiling, speaking, and even touching a person sometimes. It wasn't so bad when she touched a woman on the shoulder, but she'd patted men on the shoulder, too, especially those who worked for her in the kitchen.

She had never touched the big man, though. All of their foreplay had been with their eyes. That was really upsetting, for some reason. That guy spit on the sidewalk. He blew his nose on his fingers. Disgusting! Then he came into the kitchen and touched food! Anna permitted it. People ate that food. Oh, she was picky about the way a meal looked on a plate, but unconcerned that those fancy radishes and greenery were contaminated with germs from the scum who fingered them.

The plan originally had been to eliminate homeless bums from Tulsa. But things had changed. Anna would be next to die.

Chapter Seven

Anna hated leaving the mission late at night. The day had been busier than usual. After the people were gone, she and Rosie had huddled in the back office proofreading and perfecting a grant that needed to be postmarked by midnight. Writing the project had gone well and Anna felt good about it. The mission might pick up some much-needed federal money.

The two left together and walked to Rosie's car, which was closest. Anna had been forced to park a block away when she came back from the veterinarian. Rosie taxied her to her Civic and Anna was glad she didn't have to walk the dark streets alone.

Her Honda started immediately. She smiled gratefully, turned on her headlights and waved goodbye to Rosie, who then drove on down the street toward the post office. The snow had stopped so she didn't have to scrape the windshield. She let her car warm for a minute and entertained herself by blowing white puffs of breath into the cold air. The late night darkness spooked her. She put her car into gear and pulled away from the curb slowly, being careful not to spin her tires on the snow-packed street.

It would be good to get home and take a hot shower. Her clothes smelled of dog and the remnants of supper—cabbage and beef. She longed to scrub herself clean, slip on soft flannel pajamas and wrap herself in the fleecy robe that Rosie had given her for Christmas.

"Came from Wally-World," Rosie had said with a laugh. "It's your favorite colors—red and white—just perfect for watching games and cheering on the Sooners." And it was. There were no games on tonight, but she had plans that involved an exciting mystery and a cup of Earl Grey tea. She smiled at the thought. Heavenly.

Anna drove to I-244 east and then eased her way into the traffic. Music from 88.7 kept her company. Her mind drifted. Gus wasn't a street person. He was a cop and his real name probably wasn't even Gus. She sort of hated that fact. She'd grown fond of the moniker.

The man had resurrected emotions she hadn't felt for years. She might regret getting her hopes up about him, but decided to push past her fears. Maybe it was time for an adventure. And she really liked the guy.

For the first time in years she felt truly happy. Soon she would be home. The traffic was light and the road was familiar. She drove with what she called "automatic pilot," enjoying her own thoughts. Suddenly headlights blazed in her rearview mirror, dazzling her. She switched to the night mirror then watched a dark colored pickup pull just inches from her bumper.

Anna gripped the steering wheel and moved to the right, forgetting it was a merging lane that would fast disappear. The pickup followed her, still on her bumper. What was wrong with this person? She glanced into the rearview mirror and could see nothing but the truck's outline. What was happening?

"Pass, will you? Pass and leave me alone." Should she pull off the road and let the maniac go by? What if he did the same? She'd read about such things in the paper. Fear tightened her muscles and made her heart beat faster.

Could this be an abduction? Road rage? Had she passed the truck in oblivion and cut the driver off?

Suddenly the pickup pulled into the left lane and she went weak with relief. *Finally.* He was passing. Then without warning, the truck sideswiped her small Civic bumping the car toward a sharp incline. Anna liked her tiny Civic's economy, but suddenly wished she'd gotten an older big car—a Cadillac or Buick—or maybe a pickup.

My God, she thought. *I'm going off the road.* Everything turned to slow motion. Her car shuddered and started down the embankment. Another bump from the pickup skidded her car sideways and she knew it would roll. She gripped the wheel and prayed, *help me, help me, help me,* wondering what dying might be like. The car tipped, rolled and landed on the passenger's side, the headlights still on.

It was a minute before Anna could think. Her body felt bruised and she was hanging by her seatbelt, legs braced against the floorboard.

I'm alive. Thank God, I'm alive.

Her shoulder hurt where it strained against the belt and the engine was still running. She smelled gasoline. Oh my God! She had to get out of the car. She felt for the key and switched it off. The engine shuddered and stopped. She reached for the belt release, then paused. She had to think—she couldn't lose her nerve or she might burn alive. She took a firm hold on the wheel with her left hand then released her seatbelt with her right.

Her legs and body fell toward the passenger door, but she held on in an attempt to keep herself upright. Her feet sank into water and she realized that she had settled into a creek of some kind. She moved her foot and freezing water seeped through her athletic shoe and wet her sock.

She pulled on the driver's door handle but it wouldn't open. The wreck must have jammed it. "Think!" she said aloud. "Think!"

She struggled to open the glove compartment and find something to break the window. Her fingers grasped her four-battery Mag-Lite. Anna turned her face away from the glass and swung with all of her might. She heard the pane shatter. "Thank you Jesus for safety glass," she said.

Anna turned sideways and tried to slip her torso up through the window, but her puffy coat stopped her. She wiggled out of the sleeves and tried again. A wrenching pain shot through her and she realized she'd injured some ribs. Ignoring the pain, she braced one foot against the seat and heaved herself upward, snaking her upper body through the window until her rump rested on the sill. She bent her knees and her feet found purchase on the armrest.

She rested for a moment and the smell of gasoline grew stronger, sending terror through her veins and giving her new strength. Using her legs she heaved herself over the driver's side door, down the roof of the car, and fell into the creek. The icy water soaked half of her body before she got her feet under her. The wind blew against her wet clothes and she knew she could die of hypothermia. She struggled to her feet, edged around the car, and reached through the window for her coat, pulling it part way up before it snagged on something.

A car door slammed up on the highway and her heart froze. Was he coming after her, or could it be a Good Samaritan? Anna let go of her coat and moved away from the car and into the darkness. As silently as possible, she crouched in some underbrush, thanking God that the city hadn't had enough funds to turn on the roadway lights.

A single figure started down the embankment, partly walking, partly sliding. The night was dark and the moon hidden behind a cloud. All Anna could see was a figure made bulky by a heavy winter coat. His face was covered by a ski mask, and she knew for sure he was trying to kill her. She thought for a minute she might vomit. The figure paused and studied the car. Anna saw that her discarded coat was jumbled against the wheel, looking as if it might be an incapacitated driver.

The figure reached into his pocket and made a quick movement. She smelled sulfur and saw a small flame. A quick flick spun the match toward the car. Anna tried to make herself as small as possible.

Fire leaped upward from the leaking gasoline and mushroomed into a blazing inferno. The figure then turned and walked back up the hill.

Oh my God! Anna cowered in the darkness, her heart pounding, praying she wouldn't be noticed. She wasn't sure how long she huddled in the creek bed. Finally, she realized her feet were turning to ice. She smelled the weeds and the dirt and the fire. She looked toward the car and saw the nearby winter grass catch fire and begin moving toward her.

She struggled to her feet. Pain shot through her shoulder. She half walked, half ran away from the flames. Anna had never been so cold in her life. She didn't dare walk toward the highway, so she decided to go the opposite direction. She looked up and saw lights in the distance. Hope fueled her energy and she kept moving. She crossed a field and could see the outline of a house. She'd moved past the road and was looking up toward a house. Frigid air burned her lungs but she had to get to the house and ring a bell. She was so tired.

She had to keep walking. Up through the weeds she crawled, too tired to worry about any danger—broken glass, old tin cans with razor sharp edges—she must keep moving. Inch by inch she struggled forward. Her crawl seemed to take forever. Her fingers clutched the twisted wires of a chain link fence. Relief surged, then dismay. Her strength was gone. Her limbs seemed to have turned into ice. How on earth would she get over this barrier?

A dog began to bark. The animal was in the yard—she could smell him—a wet, doggy smell that made her heart jump into her throat. She knew that dogs in this area were often kept for safety and that she might be attacked. She also knew that she had to get in out of the cold.

Anna grabbed the fence, gathered the strength she had left and pulled herself upright. She opened her mouth to call for help, but couldn't force a sound from her lips.

The moon came from behind the clouds and she saw that next to this fence was an eight foot privacy fence. She had no choice. She had to climb the links, get past the barking dog and pound on the back door. Her arms seemed to belong to someone else. Her legs trembled from the cold and from shock.

I can do this! Anna told herself. *I must do this.*

She gathered the last of her strength, lifted her leg and got a toe-hold in the wire, raised her torso upward and then swung a leg over the fence. She heaved herself over the top bar and hit the ground on her right knee, then flopped onto her face. She lay still, dazed and hurting.

A dog was on top of her, barking and slapping her in the face with something wet. It was a minute before she realized he wasn't slapping her, but licking her.

"Nice doggy," she said in a voice she didn't recognize. "Nice doggy."

Light flooded the yard and the back door swung open.

"Hey, Mopar! Quit that barking! What's going on out there?"

Anna looked toward a man standing on the back porch step and caught her breath. He had a gun pointed toward her. She raised her hands toward him.

"Don't shoot. Please don't shoot." Her voice was so weak she wondered if he could hear. What was the use? She dropped her arms, exhausted and terrified. She lay her head down on the snow covered grass, too tired and too cold to worry about dying.

Chapter Eight

Everything turned fuzzy. A man and a woman shouted back and forth, and then the man lifted Anna from the hard ground and carried her into a warm house where he set her in a soft-as-butter chair. The frantic sounding woman spoke on the telephone, but Anna scarcely noticed. Her attention was on the blankets being wrapped around her. After the chair was pushed into a reclining position she closed her eyes, longing for sleep.

"What happened, ma'am," he asked. "Did you have an accident? Is someone chasing you?"

She wanted to answer but the words wouldn't form. She must have dozed off because sirens awakened her, screaming in the background. The man and woman fussed over her, coaxing her to sip from a cup and asking questions she was too sleepy to answer. The same wretched dog barked and barked and barked, even when he was scolded.

"Quiet, Mopar," the man ordered. Anna wondered who on earth would name an animal Mopar.

The woman asked her a question and she opened her mouth to speak, but said "Thank you," instead of telling them her name as requested.

"She must be in shock," the man said. "Let her sleep, the police are coming."

"Thank you," Anna mumbled once more.

Sometime later she dreamed that Gus was calling her name. His hands stroked her hair and touched her cheek and it felt heavenly.

"Anna," he said. "Anna, you must wake up."

Suddenly sleep was gone but Gus stayed, kneeling beside her. "Wake up, Anna," he said again. "The ambulance is here. They're taking you to the emergency room."

Anna blinked. He was there in this house of strangers. She looked up into his worried blue eyes and felt safe again. A couple of uniformed patrol officers stood by the door along with the plainclothes detective who had tried to arrest Gus outside the mission.

"You're really here?" she asked, knowing that if Gus was here as a cop then his cover had been blown. How on earth would the police stop the killer? Was that her fault?

Gus cupped her chin in his hands and looked into her eyes. "I'm not a street person, Anna. I'm a policeman. My name is Mike Sanders and I was undercover at the mission investigating the murders. A patrolman saw your car burning beside the highway. He called it in and ran your tag. Do you think you're up to telling us what happened?"

"I'll try." Her head began to clear. "Would you help me sit up?"

Mike put his hand to the side of the chair and moved the mechanism, gently raising her to a sitting position.

"How are you feeling? Would you like to go to the hospital before we talk?"

Anna shifted her weight in the chair to test how she felt. Everything hurt, especially her ribs, but she didn't want to go to the hospital. She hated hospitals, especially emergency rooms. She'd be there all night.

"No. No hospital."

He argued with her a minute then relented.

"All right, all right. Do you feel able ride to the police station? We need to ask questions and get a statement. I can always take you to the hospital later if you change your mind."

"Of course, I'm fine," Anna lied, wondering if she could even stand much less walk. But she managed both, mostly from pure determination.

The ordeal at the police station seemed to go on forever, but Gus stayed with her. His presence was like an anchor in a storm. He ran interference for her, fielding questions from Detective Sanchez who called him Mike.

Mike. His name was Mike. It suited, but she liked Gus better.

The police wanted to know every detail about what had happened. Who was around the mission when she and Rosie had left? Had she seen anyone following before she was on I-244? The questions went on and on. Her brain seemed to lock up with the barrage.

Gus held up his hand for silence and spoke to her in a quiet voice. "Take some deep breaths, Anna, and ground yourself. Relax for a minute." He took her hand and held it gently. "Picture something that calms you."

She pictured her grandma's kitchen—the ages-old white Magic Chef stove with one burner that no longer worked, African violets blooming in the window over the sink, the comfortable clutter of a meal-in-progress. She smelled cinnamon and apples and the rich aroma of roasting pork. MeeMaw stood at the counter shaping pie dough with an ancient rolling pin that had lost one handle before Anna was even born. Her body relaxed.

"Think back to when you locked the back door at the mission. Keep your eyes closed and visualize the drive minute by minute. Tell us what happened," Gus said.

For a minute she resisted shifting scenes inside her head. She didn't want to leave her childhood memories. Gus' fingers closed gently around her hand. She took a deep breath and brought her mind back to the near present. She thought for a minute and then recounted exactly what had happened, step by step. The warmth of Gus close by kept her calm until she reached the road attack. Panic hit. Words stuck in her throat and she stopped.

After a brief pause Gus said. "You can do this, Anna. I know you can."

Anna opened her eyes, looked first at Gus and then at the other detective. She took another breath, then slowly recounted each terrifying minute of the attack and her flight to safety.

"Why would anyone want to kill me?" she asked. "Was it some kind of road rage?" The officers exchanged a glance. Rodriguez raised an eyebrow and Gus sighed.

"We don't know," he said. "It could have been road rage. Did you cutoff this guy, or refuse to let him into your lane? Anything, even something small that would have triggered such anger?"

Anna frowned, trying to think. Then she shook her head.

"I don't know. It had been a long day and I was on automatic pilot. I don't think so, but I couldn't swear to it."

"Folks need to pay more attention to their driving," Sanchez snapped. "That's what causes accidents."

"She wasn't the one who drove someone off the road," Gus retorted.

"You like the other possibility better?" Sanchez asked.

"What possibility?" Anna turned her gaze toward Officer Sanchez.

"Okay, I think that's enough." Gus spoke in an even tone but Anna saw the glance he shot at Sanchez. "We're all getting tired. I'll take Anna home. She can come back tomorrow to sign her statement."

Gus drove her home in a black Ford Explorer that she figured was his personal car. The car was well cared for but looked lived in. A traveling coffee cup rested in the holder, sunglasses were in the side pocket along with a copy of today's *Tulsa World*.

They drove for about five minutes before he spoke. "You hungry?"

"No," Anna said. Then her stomach rumbled. "Maybe," she corrected.

Gus grinned and shot her a concerned glance. "Look. Is there anything you'd like to ask me? You've been through a lot today."

It was a minute before she spoke.

"Is it okay if I keep on calling you Gus? I know it's not your name, but I kind of like it."

Chapter Nine

That was the last question on earth Mike had expected. Women. With everything that had happened she wanted to know if she could call him Gus.

"Sure, you can call me Gus." He didn't care what she called him, just as long as she smiled at him while she spoke. It was pure luck that he'd been at the station updating Sanchez about his undercover work when they'd heard the call that a red Honda Civic just off the road was burning. He'd known the accident had been on her route home.

Dread had drained through him and his heart had turned to ice. The thought of her hurt, or dead, had made him want to howl with rage.

"That could be Anna Rainwater. I'm going out to check," Mike said.

Rodriguez grabbed his own coat and trailed after him. "Can't we just wait to hear by radio? Even if it is her, a wreck wouldn't have anything to do with the murders we're investigating."

"I'm not so sure," he'd called back.

Anna's voice brought him back to the present.

"I live in southeast Tulsa," she said.

"Wouldn't you rather go to a friend's house? How about Rosie? I don't think you should be alone. You've had a shock. Someone needs to keep an eye on you."

"She doesn't have room. Her mother and three grandchildren live with her, and there are only three small bedrooms."

"Her mother? Really?"

"Yeah, she's 83 and still going strong. She looks after the kids while Rosie works. I'll be okay at home."

He knew she was lying. "Sorry, I can't do that. But don't worry. I'm taking you to a place where you'll be safe. We need to talk—to sort through a few things away from the shelter." Mostly he just wanted her near him.

Anna opened her mouth to protest and then closed it. The truth was she didn't want to go home. She didn't want to be alone. Someone had tried to kill her and she was scared and confused. She would have asked to be taken to a hotel or motel, but couldn't afford one. She sat quietly and watched him drive. He steered the car with a focus that gave her confidence. She saw the barely noticeable movement of his eyes as he checked the rearview mirror and scanned the area around them. Suddenly she felt safe.

He turned on 15th Street and headed through a neighborhood close to Tulsa University. Most of the houses in this area had been built during the 1920's and 1930's. Anna had always liked this part of town, but Kevin had preferred a newer and much fancier house on the south side of town. Their house had had all the bells and whistles that money could buy, but no real hominess. She actually preferred her current place, a small tract house in a working class neighborhood. She'd furnished the place with pieces from garage sales and newspaper ads, then lined the walls with shelves she nailed together herself, and filled them with her books.

Gus turned right. "Where are you taking me?" she asked.

"Home with me." He glanced at her. "Don't worry, I'm not going to hit on you. I only want to help."

"To protect and serve," Anna said with a smile.

Gus laughed. "Yeah. That's the oath I took."

She saw a flash of what looked like wistfulness on his face, then just as quickly the look was gone, hidden behind his cop's mask. Anna wondered what that might mean, if anything.

Gus turned into the drive of a white bungalow that Anna guessed had been built during Tulsa's first oil boom. The yard could have used a bit of TLC, but the house had fresh white paint with yellow trim. He drove down a longish drive and parked in a detached garage.

"Let me get out first and check things over," he said.

Anna caught her breath. He expected danger? Could someone have followed them? She turned in her seat and perused the area, now illuminated by automatic yard lights. He walked around to her side of the car and opened the door.

"Everything's okay." He looked down at her. "Hey, don't be scared. I always check things out—it's an ingrained habit." He took her arm and helped her out.

She couldn't remember the last time a man had done that—if ever.

"Come on in. I have some leftover barbecue in the freezer that we can have for supper. I charcoaled it on the grill and it's not too bad."

"You saved barbeque from last summer? That's what I call willpower. I would have eaten that by October at least."

"I've got no willpower when it comes to barbeque," Gus said with a laugh. "I charcoaled it on Christmas Eve."

"But there was a blizzard on Christmas Eve."

"Yeah. But we all have our holiday traditions. So I bundled up and barbequed."

Had he spent Christmas alone? She had to know.

"I'm sure your family was grateful for your wintertime sacrifice."

"Naw, it was just me. I never take off at Christmas. I volunteer so the guys with kids can be home. It was just me."

His consideration impressed Anna. And barbequing made perfect sense to her. It was the sort of thing she might have done if she'd had to celebrate alone. She would have faced freezing weather and blowing snow and shouted inside her own head, *See, I am too having a good time. I can be happy all by myself.'*

Anna glanced at him and he grinned. A sort of electricity shot through her body making her giddy with happiness. She watched him unlock a deadbolt on the backdoor and swing it open.

"Welcome," he said.

Anna stepped through the back door and breathed in the lingering odor of fried onions and eggs and the oldness of the house. The kitchen hadn't been remodeled in years—maybe never. The cabinets were low, as if built for a petite housewife from the past. The stove looked like MeeMaw's. The only new thing was a stainless steel, double door refrigerator. She hid a smile and guessed it was filled with his favorite kind of beer.

"This is nice," she said. "Really nice. I love old houses."

He didn't speak for a minute, just looked at her with appreciation in his eyes. She smiled up at him, then shivered.

"Hey, you're freezing. I'll turn up the furnace. The house is small so it doesn't take but a few minutes to warm up."

Anna felt him take her arm and propel her forward through a small dining room and into the living room. He grabbed a rainbow colored afghan from a chair and wrapped it around her, then lifted her in his arms and placed her on an overstuffed sofa. Suddenly he was gone and she missed his touch.

An instant later he was back with what looked like a handmade comforter—squares from old wool and denim and corduroy—sewn together and tied with yarn. Similar to one she had inherited from MeeMaw.

"Does your quilt tell a story?" Anna asked before she thought.

"A story?"

Anna shrugged. "I have one very like it that my grandmother made. Every square had its own story. Whether it had been a skirt or trousers or a dress. The history of who had worn the garment and who it had been passed down to, sometimes for several generations."

Gus sat on the sturdy-looking coffee table facing her and his blue eyes seemed to pierce her heart. She wished she knew what he was thinking.

"No," he said finally. "If the quilt had stories, I never heard them." He paused for a minute. "That would have been nice, though."

Chapter Ten

Next morning Anna pulled into her parking spot behind the shelter just as the sun peeked over the top of Tulsa's skyline. When dozens of folks are counting on you for food, there can be no days off. She wore Gus' down coat. It was warmer than her own, and still held his scent. He'd mooched a loaner from some guy who owned a used car lot. The big sedan was ten years old, but seemed to run all right. She might just buy it since she had carried no comprehensive on her Civic. All in all, for the first time since she had been a child, she felt looked after—cherished almost. And she liked the feeling.

Last night Mike gave her his own bed—said the mattress was new—said it was the best he had to offer. Her first impulse had been to protest, then something told her to be gracious and allow him to pamper her. The bed was soft beyond belief and filled with his presence. She could see wrinkles left by his body from the last time he'd slept there. The shape of his head still showed on the pillow and the faint essence of his body was both disturbing and intoxicating. Even with bruises and aching muscles she had slept like a baby.

She had smiled all the way to work, last night's attack pushed to the back of her mind. Her aching body felt much better this morning. She turned off the engine and noticed Rosie hadn't yet arrived. That was good. Her friend needed to spend more time with her family.

Anna opened the car door and stepped out of the car just as Rex Martin's white van pulled up. He waved at her.

"Hi there, Annie," Rex said. "I heard on the news that a cook from a soup kitchen had been run off the road. I figured it had to be you, and I knew you'd come in to work no matter what. Are you okay?"

Anna shrugged and smiled. "I think so, just a little sore in places. But I'd rather not talk about last night, just now. It's still too soon."

"Then I won't pump you with questions. I'm glad you're here. I just got a call from a supermarket in Sand Springs. They have some produce to donate. The store rejected it, something about the truck's refrigeration unit getting messed up and the merchandise wilting."

"Yeah!" Anna forced herself to be enthusiastic. "I'll bet I can salvage most of it. Just bring everything in. I'm going to start a big vat of pinto beans for lunch." Drooping and shop worn produce was her forte. MeeMaw had shown Anna years ago how to bring tired looking vegetables back to life. A quick soak in ice water always did the trick.

"There's half a semi full. There won't be room for everything in my van and I want to make sure we get the best." Rex hung his head and shuffled his feet. "I'm really sorry, but I need you to go with me, you're better than me at picking the best produce."

Anna sighed. He was right and the kitchen really needed fresh vegetables. "Give me a couple of minutes. I'll go inside and put the beans on to simmer, leave a note for the guys, and be right with you."

Rex looked at his watch and shifted his shoulders. "I'm in kind of a hurry," he said. "There's a lot going on today down at my store."

Anna hesitated. The guy donated his time and energy while she was paid for her efforts. He was the one who should call the shots.

"Okay, I'll make goulash today—that will be fast. I'll do the beans tomorrow." She'd call Rosie on the way and tell her what was going on.

Rex had left the engine running and the smell of exhaust fumes choked Anna. She breathed through her mouth to keep from gagging and climbed in. At least it was warm inside.

"Whew, it feels good in here. This is the worst winter we've had in awhile." She smiled at Rex. "Where's Gladys this morning?"

It was a minute before Rex answered and Anna shot him a look from the corner of her eye.

"I didn't go by and pick her up. We're having some problems." Rex cleared his throat. "I thought maybe I could talk to you about it."

Now what, she wondered? Anna had an uneasy feeling that she was about to be given information that she didn't want. The last thing she was in the mood for was a blow-by-blow description of someone else's personal problems. Goodness knew, she had enough of her own, and she sure didn't want to compare war stories with Rex. She took a deep breath.

"Look Rex. I like both you and Gladys." A stretch of the truth, but what else could she say? "If you're having relationship troubles, then Gladys is the one you need to talk to. I make it a rule never to interfere in friends' love lives," she spoke bluntly and then changed the subject. "I'd better call Rosie and let her know where I am." She reached down for her purse. "This is going to be one busy day," she said, "but I'm grateful for the donated food."

Rex remained silent and seemed totally immersed in his driving. No wonder Gladys seems so odd, Anna thought. The woman probably gets tired of talking to herself.

Anna noticed they were headed south instead of west as she had expected. "Hey, I thought we were going to Sand Springs."

"Prattville," Rex said, his voice gruff and self conscious sounding. "I know where I'm going."

Now she'd hurt his feelings. What if he stopped bringing food?

"Sorry about the backseat driving. I had a miserable night." Might as well try to get back on his good side,

Anna thought. She turned toward him. "If you still want to talk I'll be happy to listen."

Rex seemed to relax. "I had a bad night, too." His voice softened as he pulled off Riverside Drive onto I-44. "The light of day makes me think I maybe made a mistake."

Ah. Now comes the sad story of his crumbling relationship with Gladys. She'd listen and give the old sympathetic emotional grunt. That was all anyone wanted—not advice.

"Every relationship has problems," Anna spoke kindly. "Usually it's best to just wait a couple of days and see if things get better."

"I'm not sure I want things to get better between Gladys and me." He shot a rather pinched look at Anna, causing a shiver to slide through her body. "I'm thinking that maybe there's someone better for me." Rex waited, as if to get up his courage.

Another shiver ran down Anna's spine. Had she opened a can of worms? Could he be thinking about hitting on *her*?

"You probably should sleep on things a few more days. Make sure this is what you really want." She saw his mouth open to protest and she cut him off. "I don't think I'll ever have another relationship, myself."

An image of Gus rose in her mind, and she knew she was lying.

"The right man could change that," Rex said, his voice thick with self-consciousness.

"No chance," Anna lied, then again reached into her purse for her phone. The cell wasn't in the side pocket where it was supposed to be and self-annoyance rippled through her. She'd been thinking of something else and had dropped it into the wrong place. A favorite trick. Her fingers rummaged through the voluminous bag and finally touched her phone. Anna breathed a sigh of relief and started to dial.

Unexpectedly Rex swerved sharply to the right. The truck hit a pothole and Anna lurched against the seatbelt. Rex reached to steady her and his hand clipped the phone, knocking it to the floor. He braked unexpectedly and the phone disappeared under the seat.

"Damned potholes! I try to miss them, but they're everywhere." Rex took Anna's hand and squeezed her fingers. "Are you all right?"

Anna hadn't seen any potholes but her focus had been on the cell. Was he lying? Trying to force her to listen to his tale of woe? Hoping to date her?

"I'm okay, but I need my phone." Anna reached to unfasten her seatbelt but Rex's hand stopped her. She pulled away from his touch and shivered again.

"I don't allow anyone to unbuckle while my car is moving. It's illegal and too dangerous on the highway. Anyway, you'll need a flashlight to be able to see under the seat." He turned off the road and headed north to 51st Street where he turned back west.

"Isn't it quicker to drive through Berryhill?" Anna asked.

"I've got to make a quick stop near here. You don't mind, do you? It won't take a minute, and you'll get to see my cabin." Rex turned right and then, soon after, left.

"Your cabin?" Anna scanned the deserted area. Pin oaks and bramble and heavy undergrowth crowded the fields. "I'm really short on time. I have to get back to the mission and cook lunch. Can't we just pick up the food?" A shiver trembled through Anna and she frowned.

Rex wheeled the van onto a trail that was barely visible from the country road. Only a person familiar with the area would know it was there.

"Please turn around and drive to Prattville," Anna said, "I'm not comfortable with going into the country."

She was beginning to doubt if there was a truck to unload. Rex seemed more interested in getting her alone than anything else.

"We're almost there. You're going to like this." Rex made another sharp turn, drove about 400 feet and stopped at a sprawling and modern-looking log cabin. "I own my house in town plus this country place," he said. "Come inside, I want you to see it. It's nice. Really nice."

Things were out of hand and Anna wasn't sure how it had happened. She looked at Rex. Yesterday she'd have described him as medium tall, slender, and physically inactive. Today, even through his wool coat, she noticed that his shoulders were well developed. The guy lifted and carried heavy boxes and wouldn't need to work out to be strong.

Rex shot her a shy smile, his eyes hopeful and childlike. Anna sighed. Her damned Irish imagination! What on earth was she thinking? This was *Rex*. The most harmless man in the world. So he had a crush on her. She'd just have to be as kind as possible and let him down easy. But damn, it was embarrassing.

"You go in and get what you need. Let's don't have any more personal conversations until we've reached town." She met his gaze and his eyes hardened at her answer. Anna took a deep breath. "Please remember that Gladys is my friend, too."

Rex relaxed and his eyes softened. "I'll bring a flashlight back with me so I can get your cell from under the seat." He jumped out of the van and headed toward the house.

Anna unfastened her seatbelt and fished under the seat. Her fingers touched something metal. She leaned in closer and grasped the shaft of a flashlight. Had Rex forgotten he had stashed one? She pulled it out, opened her door and stepped onto the snow covered ground.

She switched on the light and looked under the seat. Her heart stopped beating.

An old ice pick and a package of chocolate covered mints lay next to her phone.

Chapter Eleven

Anna froze in place. Who did this stuff belong to? Rex? That couldn't be. Gladys maybe? Had he discovered these things and didn't have the heart to turn Gladys over to the police? Was that what he wanted to talk about?

It was a minute before Anna could react. She had to get away from here—hide—or run. If she took the road he could follow in his pickup. On foot she might outrun him.

Pin oaks, heavily laden with snow, might have been good cover in the summertime, but it was winter and much of their foliage was on the ground. Plus her tracks in the snow would be a dead giveaway. Her only chance was speed.

She sprinted away from the cabin and into the woods, ignoring the pain in her ribs. She'd heard of people pushing past their pain, but that wasn't true for her. She hurt like hell. Freezing wind whipped through her coat and burned her lungs, making her struggle for each breath.

A yell of fury—animalistic and inhuman—sounded from the direction of the house. Oh God! He was the killer! He'd be on top of her in a flash. She had seen a mobile home along the road, but where was it? The van changed directions so many times that she had lost count. Still, the general direction had stayed pretty much the same. If she headed southwest it was possible she might find the mobile home.

But what if there were children there—alone with their mother or even by themselves? She couldn't put anyone else in danger. She'd forget the trailer and head for 51st street. That up and down strip of asphalt had a steady stream of traffic. It was her best chance.

MeeMaw's voice was suddenly in her head, reminding her of how Indians ran long distances. She forced herself to relax and to fall into a steady rhythm, ignoring the pain. She dodged between the trees and felt she was doing well. She could do this. Then her foot hit a rock, her ankle twisted and she fell to the ground. Pain shot through her ankle and she tried to stand. Damn, but it hurt.

Anna saw a barbed wire fence a few feet ahead and a sick disappointment drained through her. She limped forward realizing that her luck had run out. Then she heard a whinny and a pinto pony tossed his mane and trotted toward her. She held her breath. Maybe she could catch the horse and ride him to safety.

The feat would have been a cinch when she was in her teens. But it had been a lifetime since she'd ridden a horse without a saddle, much less without a bridle. Growing up she'd done it many times on MeeMaw's small farm. Could she manage such a feat all these years later?

The horse walked toward her, friendly and curious. He seemed to be comfortable around people. Drawing from her memory, Anna made comforting noises in her throat that she had learned years ago. She spoke gently, "Hello pretty one. Want to take a little ride? You're a sweetheart."

The animal leaned across the fence and nuzzled her neck. "Okay, baby, let me see if I can use this wire fence for a ladder. Then I won't have to worry about getting up onto your back." She grasped his mane and put her foot on the middle wire. The horse shied away, but Anna held on. Barbs scissored into her flesh but she managed to swing one leg over the fence and grab the mane with her other hand. The pinto kept backing away, pulling Anna with him, making her body a bridge between the fence and the horse. The sharp wire dug deeper into her flesh and she felt blood run down her leg. But she ignored her pain and kept murmuring.

"It's okay, it's okay." She wished she knew the horse's name. He tossed his head trying to escape, but she held fast.

Footsteps crunched behind her and fear blitzed through her.

"Anna," Rex yelled.

It was now or never. Gathering her strength, she catapulted herself forward, landing across the horse on her belly and jarring her ribs. "Oh God!" she moaned, praying she didn't faint. The horse whinnied and struggled against her weight.

"Easy, boy," she said. "Easy there." She swung herself sideways and threw her leg over the horse. Adjusting her grip on his mane, she prodded him with her heels and he galloped forward. Anna slid sideways, and for one awful moment she thought she'd be thrown to the ground. But her fingers kept a death hold on the mane and she managed to right herself and grip the animal with her legs.

Screams of rage reached her through the freezing wind as she raced away, using her legs to guide the pony. Thank God she'd made it.

Anna leaned against the horse's neck to escape the wind and headed south. Her body hurt so badly she could hardly breathe. Suddenly she remembered that if she took the pony off the owner's land, she could be arrested for horse stealing. But that seemed like a small problem.

She rode for what she thought was about three miles before another barbed wire fence stopped her. She slid off the horse and tried to crawl through the fence, holding down the middle wire. Her down coat caught on the barbs above and trapped her. Panic turned her muscles to jelly. Then she remembered that Rex was miles behind her. She took as deep a breath as possible and pulled with all of her might. Fabric ripped and feathers flew—but she was on the other side.

Stunned by pain for a minute, Anna's mind went blank and her sense of direction spun out of whack. Precious moments ticked by. Bent double, gasping for air, her hands resting on her knees, she pictured MeeMaw shelling peas on the back porch steps. Anna's entire body ached and her ankle hurt like hell. But pain had never stopped her MeeMaw. She reminded herself that she was Cherokee.

Anna limped in the direction she hoped was east and stumbled out of the woods and onto a dirt road, relieved to see its smoother surface. Then fear struck again. What if Rex had gone back to get his van?

Making a split decision, Anna headed south down the road. Her ankle wouldn't last another five minutes running in the woods. She forced herself into a slow but steady lope, stiffening her leg to help minimize the agony. Still pain wracked through her when she put weight on her ankle. But she ran on. Cold wind burned her lungs and she panted for breath. Her foot gave way and she fell to the snow packed ground. Every part of her body hurt and tears stung her eyes. What was the use? She just kept falling. She closed her eyes in despair and suddenly felt warmer.

MeeMaw's tales of their ancestors freezing to death came to mind. Never stop moving, MeeMaw had said. If you rest, you die. Anna forced her elbows beneath her and pushed upward. She got a knee under her and struggled to her feet. Her heart sank when she saw that she faced another damned hill.

Keep on trying! MeeMaw's voice was in her head, cheering her on. Pulling strength from somewhere beyond herself, Anna put one foot in front of the other and dragged herself to the top of the rise. She heard a vehicle in the distance and turned to see Rex's white van at the top of a far hill.

Anna turned and ran blindly, agony tearing at her body. She stumbled and almost fell, but forced herself to press on. Her toe caught on a hard edge and she sprawled forward, scraping her elbows and then her chin, just as tires squealed. Anna looked up and saw a pickup skidding toward her, only then aware that she'd reached 51st street. "Help me God," she prayed and then scrunched her eyes shut, rolling away from the oncoming tires. When she opened them she saw a truck wheel about six inches from her head.

Doors slammed and a child's voice shrilled through the cold air. "Hey, Dad, that lady forgot to look both ways before crossing the highway."

"Get back in the truck," a man's voice shouted.

Anna felt herself being lifted to her feet and steadied by a strong arm. "What the hell were you thinking, lady? I almost ran over you."

"There's a killer after me in a white van," she gasped. "I'm not crazy—he really is. Get your kids away from here so he can't hurt them. Then call the police."

"I *am* the police. I'm an off duty Tulsa cop." His voice sounded confident but Anna knew danger was upon them.

She pointed toward the van racing off the country road.

"Look out," she shouted. Anna grabbed the man's arm and leaped to safety, pulling him with her.

She caught a glimpse of Rex hunched behind the wheel, his face red and furious—almost unrecognizable. The van rocked from side to side, barely missing the cop's pickup. It whipped to the right and slid down the embankment then smashed into a tree.

The off-duty policeman shouted for his kids to get on the floorboard then pulled a gun from under his coat. He ran down to the van, opened the door and hauled Rex out. Anna's head was spinning but she managed to limp to the truck. She spotted a bright haired boy who held a cell phone.

"I've got 911," he said.

"Ask them to notify Detective Mike Sanders of the Tulsa Police," Anna managed to gasp.

Chapter Twelve

Hours later Mike drove Anna back to his house and fed her hot soup. Then he bundled her in his hand-tied patchwork comforter and tucked her into his bed. It never occurred to her to protest. More than anything else she wanted to be near him. Instantly she drifted into sleep.

The smell of coffee awakened her the next morning. Her clothes were on a small table, clean and neatly folded. Anna reached for her sweatshirt and held the garment to her nose, breathing in the clean fragrance. Warmth sprung up in her heart and spread through her chest. Washing and drying her clothes while she slept was the most romantic thing any man had ever done for her. It even beat a dozen roses.

Anna slid out of bed, pulled off the t-shirt Gus had loaned her for a nightgown, and threw it on the bed post. She dressed, then finger-combed her hair before stepping into the kitchen where Gus was flipping pancakes.

The look of her unnerved him. Sleepy-eyed, with raven-colored hair cascading down her shoulders and a sweet smile on her face, she was a vision he would remember forever. He could hardly breathe.

"Anna, you're beautiful."

"I'm a wreck and I have morning-mouth," she said with a smile.

Like he cared about that? She'd just rolled out of his bed, and even though he hadn't shared it with her, just the thought of those black curls on his pillow made his knees weak. He wanted to protest—to explain that her beauty couldn't be marred by anything—but the words wouldn't come to his lips. So he just stood there, grinning like an idiot until he smelled scorching pancakes.

"Oh, crap. These are burned. I'll have to make more." He turned off the gas flame under the griddle then turned back to Anna.

"Nothing wrong with well done," she said, her gaze melding into his. She stepped toward him and he waited for her, not daring to breathe. Another minute and she'd be in his arms.

The cell clipped to his belt rang. His first impulse was to throw the blasted thing on the floor and stomp on it. He let it ring twice more before he answered.

Anna had never in her life so enjoyed watching a man talk on the phone. He spoke in monotones, annoyance showing on his face. All the while his eyes seemed to devour her. He finally ended the call.

"Rex is safely in jail. The DA says there's plenty of evidence and there's no doubt he'll be convicted."

"Good," Anna said. "That's good."

"Rosie called earlier and said for you to stay home today and rest. She's called in some markers and lined up volunteers from her church."

"Rosie's the best," she said.

What was it about this man and this kitchen that made her want to stand and just look at him? He grinned at her in comfortable silence and somewhere Anna could hear a dog bark, reminding her she needed to check on the black and white mix she'd left at the vet's.

"I still need to go in. Our main source of donation will be gone, and something else has to be arranged," she said. "But first I need to call the vet and see how my dog is getting along."

"I've already talked to Luther and he's working the phones for food donations. And don't worry about the dog. We'll pick him up this afternoon."

We? Her heart soared as if she were a teenager again. "We?" she asked softly.

"We," Gus grinned at her.

Anna chuckled, feeling warm and safe and happy. "First I have to shower. I stink."

"Yeah, I know." Mike's eyes devoured her. "You smell like horse and sweat…and woman. You smell really good—to me." He paused for a minute and grinned.

"Does that mean you don't require a perfect woman?"

"Lady, I mean that, to me, you are perfect."

Weeding Out the Problem
Peggy Moss Fielding

Peggy Moss Fielding is a native Okie who lives in Tulsa, Oklahoma. She is a full time writer with a great many books, articles and short stories to her credit. She has lived in Japan, Cuba and the Republic of the Philippines. Her most recent full length novel is titled *Scoundrels' Bargain*.

For my cousin, Julia Mae Bice Hoover,
who is, in essence, my big sister.

Chapter One

Lisa Hall backed her little Chevy into the open sided shed at the back of her Tulsa, Oklahoma property. Backing in made it easy to drive straight out and down the alley toward the main road to go teach school each morning.

Arriving at home soothed the lingering bit of irritation that old man Kelly had stirred up within her just before she'd left the school.

"Stupid bastard," Lisa muttered, and her own words made her grin. What else could he be? She wondered. Kelly was a jock, a former high school football coach who had decided that becoming a principal at an elementary school was a step up in his career climb.

Just a glance around her very own three and a half city lots and the white craftsman style house that sat in the center of the weedy yard cleared the last of her resentment for old Principal Lester's words, "Just remember young lady, you may be a hot shot first grade teacher but I'm the boss around here."

She was pretty sure the dumb jerk had farted as he talked. She hadn't *heard* anything but the smell had been overwhelming. Maybe he'd just done a job in his pants? Lisa had to giggle. She pulled off her pantyhose, stuffed them into her shoulder bag, then stepped back into her shoes and stood up from her beloved little Aveo.

She picked her way down the terraced steps to the porch at her back door. Dead grass, bushes and weeds grabbed at her skirt and her bare legs.

"I've got to do something about this. She put her bag on the porch then retraced her steps, took a short scythe from the closed side of the shed and cleared a narrow path ahead of herself as she walked back towards the concrete steps and the iron rails that led up to her back porch. She placed the scythe under the porch and promised herself she'd use the sharp tool every time she climbed up or down the weedy terraces. She should be able to keep her yard under control or, at the very least, keep her pathway reasonably clear.

Love for her old house and the big yard welled up in Lisa's chest. Her life, so far as she was concerned, was going well. She owned her house, she owned her little car, and she truly loved her first graders. Anything else was not important she thought. No man in her life? Not important. Bad boss? Ugh, but she could live with that. Old jocks were endemic in the administration areas of primary schools.

Inside her kitchen she glanced at the old fashioned wall telephone. People thought her a bit strange because she had no cell phone, but she had her reasons. A cell phone in a first grade classroom would be not just an interference, it might even cause a panic. One of the first things she did each day was collect all the children's cell phones, laptops, Nintendos or Gameboys and lock them in her private closet. A few parents had complained, but what the hell? She had to do her job and cell phone usage or electronic games weren't in any lesson plan she'd ever made. Anyway, one of the most sought after jobs in her room was "electronic monitor." That chosen child got to carry the electronic items into

Miss Hall's *private* closet—a very secret place and she or he got to do it twice a day. Yay!

A scraping sound on the kitchen stairway caused the hair on her neck to rise. Someone was out there. She tiptoed to the screen door, opened it a few inches and looked down to the left. A tall man in a white t-shirt and jeans stood at the bottom of the stairs. He had drawn her scythe from under the porch and held it in his hand.

"Hello?" She could probably slam the heavy wooden door closed before the man made it up the stairs, if he seemed threatening.

"Hello, ma'am." He held up the scythe. "I'd be willing to clean up your yard." He gestured toward the terraced pathway back of him. He stepped one step up. The odor of unwashed male wafted upward. Nothing unpleasant, just the sweat of a man who'd worked under the Oklahoma sun.

"Uh... how much?" Maybe this guy could take care of one of her problems.

The deeply tanned man smiled. Really great looking. Lisa felt a tiny clutch in her chest. That white smile seemed to beckon to her.

"How about $150 and a cold drink for the first cleanup? Then we can go down a little for a weekly once-over."

"Weekly once-over?"

"Yeah. If I come once a week the job'll get easier as the weeks go by, so I can go down on the price."

The smile again. Lisa took a deep breath. A yardman who looked like a screen star? How many gardeners in Tulsa would be able to measure up to this guy's looks?

"Did you tell me your name?"

"Zac Freeman, ma'am."

"Well, okay, Zac. We have a deal." She pointed to the shed where her car was parked. "There is a mower and also some other tools in the closed section of the shed, next to my car."

"How do I get in there? There a padlock on the shed door?"

"Key's above the door."

"You gonna tell me your name, ma'am?"

"Oh, sorry. I'm Lisa Hall."

"Fine, Miss Hall. Uh, I'd like cash if you can see to that? Got no bank account." The amazing smile flashed again. "I'll knock when I'm finished."

"Oh, I'll have to pay you tomorrow, Mr. Freeman. I don't keep much money in the house."

"Tomorrow's okay for the mowing and for the pay. How about the cool drink part of the deal?"

"Sure. Just a minute. Would Dr. Pepper be okay?" She turned toward her refrigerator. "I'll get it for you right now. It's late, nearly time for dinner. I'll put out a sandwich for you as well."

He nodded and began swinging the scythe as he walked up the path. Lisa could not tear her gaze from the broad shoulders and the nicely formed male backside. This man put every guy she knew in the shade. Wow.

Chapter Two

When the classroom door hinges creaked, the cause of the sound was preceded by the harsh odor of cigar smoke, cheap cigar smoke. Darn. Old Lester was trying to spy on her again. He thought it was his right and his duty to spy on his teachers and because their classrooms were all single portable buildings he felt free to smoke anytime he just stepped off school grounds. He always emanated "cigar." She'd give him an eyeful and an earful.

"Okay kids. Let's take a few minutes from work for our own version of The Virginia Reel." Lisa walked toward the DVD. "We need a bit of exercise." She pointed to the door where her boss lurked.

"Boys line up against the wall here in front of the door. Girls stand one girl in front of each boy." The pleased six and seven-year olds were prompt to take their places. "One of you girls will have to be a boy for this dance since Jimmy's absent today." Several girls raised hands to volunteer to be boys. "Okay, Macey. You're a boy for this reel. I'll do the calling." Lisa tapped the player and the music swelled. *Turkey in the Straw*, first, then *The Virginia Reel*, for dancing. The laughing students formed two crooked lines. Lisa tapped the DVD again for the reel.

"Bow to your partner, one and all," Lisa shouted. "Now bow to your neighbor on your left, then bow to your neighbor to your right... that means, bow to Miss Hall, kids." The loud music, the calling, and the stomping and giggling, will give that old bastard an earache. She shouted the calls in a voice that could be heard in every part of the prefab and even out on the playground.

Lisa let her consciousness wander to the man who was tending her yard today, that Zac Freeman. *I'll go by the bank and get money for him*, she promised herself. She'd need more stuff to drink as well. She couldn't wait to see the lovely male creature once again. In the meantime, old Lester was having his eardrums worked over.

Chapter Three

"Wow!" The word escaped her lips when she backed into her open shed and stood up to look at her place. The man had apparently worked like a demon. The huge yard was mowed, clipped and neatened to a fault. Her pulse raced. Not only gorgeous, but a good worker as well. He deserved his cold drink and even another sandwich. She'd throw in pickles and potato chips, she was so pleased. Better hurry. He'd probably be back anytime to collect his pay.

She took a first grade tablet and a red crayon from her attaché case. She printed *Thanks loads, Zac. Come down to the house for your cold drink,* then taped it to the shed door.

While she was putting the sandwich and chips on a paper plate she glanced up the hill through her kitchen window.

Zac was looking at the note she'd left on the shed door. He jerked the sheet from the door, then crumbled it in his big hands. No smile now. A frown creased his forehead. He smoothed the paper once again then tore it into hundreds of tiny pieces which he stuffed into his pocket, the frown still engraved on his face.

Lisa tried to recall the exact words she'd written. Had she accidently put in something offensive? No, surely not. He must be angry about something else.

Chapter Four

Lisa backed into the screen door, food in one hand, drink in the other. She looked down at Zac. Yep. Still angry.

"Hey Zac. I have money for you. The yard looks great. Are you going to be able to come to work here on a regular basis?" She hoped a compliment would drive away his fit of pique.

He nodded... still frowning. *What in the world...?*

"Zac, can we sit on the steps and I'll have a sandwich also? I have your money in my pocket. Okay?"

He nodded again. "Don't leave notes for me. Just tell me what you want done, Miss Hall."

"Lisa."

"I'll just call you Miss Hall. Don't leave notes for me. Makes me think..." he paused, "Makes me think you don't trust me to know what I'm supposed to be doing."

Oh. His male ego was involved.

She nodded. "I understand Zac... or do you want me to call you Mr. Freeman? You've done a great job here. I have your money *and* your cold drink *and* your sandwich. Do you mind eating with me?"

"Just call me Zac, but I'll call you Miss Hall since I'm just the lawn man. I don't mind eating with a pretty redhead if you can stand eating with the sweaty guy who does your yard work."

"You think I'm pretty?"

Zac took his drink and his sandwich, nodded and smiled. "I'll just eat on the bottom step. You stay up there. I sure do stink."

Oh, that big smile. Lisa resisted the urge to ask her yardman to sit on the top step with her. He had a dimple in his cheek. She hadn't seen that before. She'd tell her pal Marsha about the gorgeous gardener at school tomorrow.

Chapter Five

"Marsha, guess what! I have a yardman now," Lisa leaned toward the older teacher who was her best friend. "And, girl, he is a beautiful male for sure. He even has a dimple in one cheek. Skin like satin. A little Indian blood there, I think."

"This guy does your yard?"

"Yep. And does it beautifully, I might add. He, himself, is beautiful, Marsha. Best looking male I've seen in Tulsa, I promise you."

"Seriously?"

"Yeah. He works like a machine on that big yard of mine, and looks like he is enjoying doing the job. But darling girl, I have to tell you, he is drop dead gorgeous. Unbelievably so." She sat silent for a moment. "He wouldn't sit with me yesterday because he thought he stank. I could smell him but it wasn't bad. He's kind of touchy."

"I've been looking for someone to work on my little yard. Think your guy would come to my place?" Marsha pulled a tablet toward herself. "I'll write down my name and address for him. Do you think he'd come way over to the east side to work for me?"

"Marsha, are you trying to steal the most wonderful looking man I've ever seen, away from me?"

"I don't care what he looks like, girl. I just want someone who will work."

"Well, okay. I'll give him your address, but no smiling or sweet talk, pal. I think I want Zac for more than a yardman."

"Zac, huh?"

"Yeah, Zac Freeman. He insists on calling me *Miss* Hall. Give me your note and I'll pass it on, but no smiling or sweet talking him for sure, okay?"

"Oh, Lisa, you know I'm tangled up with Linsley Cotton and he has my complete attention. I'm not looking for another man, just a gardener."

"Well, okay. But I'm telling you the truth. I think I'm falling for Zac Freeman." She put Marsha's address into her shoulder bag. "Now I just have to get him into that mode as well."

"Would you marry a guy who stinks and cleans yards for a living?"

"Well, it's honest labor. Nothing to be ashamed of. We could give him a company name, something like 'Greenswards' or 'Yards and More,' or something, then I could say, 'My husband owns Greenswards, a gardening company.'"

"You've thought a lot about this Lisa, already talking about marriage! Are you really getting involved with this man? A yardman?"

"He thinks I'm pretty."

Chapter Six

"Well, you are kinda cute, Lisa, but never mind about your looks. What I want to hear about, is this a guy who is willing to *work*. Pretty is as pretty does, kiddo." Marsha rummaged in her purse for paper and pen. "What's his address? I'll contact him and ask him to come do my little yard."

Where did Zac live? Lisa realized she had never been given that information. The man just seemed to know when her yard needed attention. He just took care of it, named his slightly lower price each time, and, she felt, he too looked forward to the drinks and sandwiches they consumed on her back steps even though they sat several steps apart. Just thinking about perhaps seeing Zac made Lisa's breath catch. She admitted to herself that he was becoming more and more important to her.

"I don't have an address for him, Marsha. Just write him a note with your telephone and address and I'll give it to him."

The other teachers clamored to be included.

Apparently a good yardman was extremely hard to find and a man like that was desperately needed by most of her friends. Strange, the things one could learn in the teacher's lounge, especially when old Lester Kelley wasn't hanging around to put a cigar breath damper on their conversations.

Lisa collected the bits and pieces of paper which her friends handed her, then stuffed them into an old envelope that she fished from the trash basket. She'd be sure to see that Zac got all the notes. She felt thrilled, excited even, that she'd found so many new customers for him.

Chapter Seven

At home, Lisa surveyed her well-tended yard before she took the key from over the locked shed door. No taping the envelope to the shed. She'd learned her lesson there. She'd place the envelope on the mower or somewhere so Zac would be sure to find it. She couldn't wait to see him. *Come down for a sandwich* she scribbled on the envelope before she propped it against the engine casing of the mower.

Zac had seemed too shy to make a move on her. Wouldn't call her Lisa. Wouldn't sit with her. She would be the aggressor, she decided. Tonight.

What was that stuff in the corner of the dim shed? She stepped around the neatly piled bags of fertilizer and compost to see a bedroll. A shaving kit and duffel bag were nearby. A small mirror hung above his belongings. Zac was *living* in her shed? Without telling her!

Chapter Eight

Lisa glanced out her kitchen window time after time, hoping to catch Zac so she could call him down to share a hot ham and cheese sandwich and a cold Dr. Pepper with her.

I'll share something else with him also, she promised herself. *Marsha had been right when she'd said, "Sometimes the big shy guys need a little push in the right direction, girl."*

The sun was almost down when she spied her target stepping out of the locked shed, the envelope she'd left for him in his hand. He was frowning but his face didn't display anger as it had before. Actually, he looked puzzled, or perhaps "thoughtful" was the best word for his expression. Again, she felt her heart clutch at the sight of the man.

She couldn't help the huge smile that she beamed up to him. My word, that Zac was the best looking man this side of Hollywood, for sure... and he thought she was "pretty."

"Hot supper with our cold drink tonight," she called, "Grilled ham and cheese sandwiches."

"I didn't do any yard work, today, Lisa."

"Well, you still need to eat. I even have dill pickles to go with the sandwich. Is something bothering you, Zac?"

"Yeah. I don't want to get too close to you. I had a couple of beers. My breath might knock a little woman over. Don't get too close. But it's the same thing that always bothers me." He let the puzzled look disappear into a grin. "So, you found my camp? Hope you don't mind lending me a little bedroll space, Miss Hall."

"Oh, no. Did something happen to your house or apartment, Zac? I certainly don't object to your bedding down in the shed, but I have two bedrooms in my house. Your really should come on inside and sleep in my guest room and use my shower until you find a place."

Marsha's laughing voice sounded in her mind. *Uh huh, girl. Guest room. Really? You're thinking something else. I'd bet on it.*

Zac settled on the step below her. He put the envelope full of her teacher friends' requests on the step between them. He patted the envelope and cleared his throat.

"I've been living on the Tulsa streets for a long time, Miss Hall. Your shed looks like luxury accommodations to me, ma'am. Your garden hose does double duty for my shower."

"Don't you have family? What caused you to be living on the street?"

"You sure you want to hear all this? Pretty long and complicated story… or maybe not. I'll just hit the high points for you." He took a long drink and patted the envelope once again. "I'll tell you my story and then I have a confession to make."

"A confession?" She started to move down to where he sat. My word, was he married or engaged or something? "I'm willing to listen to you Zac... story and confession."

"Okay, but don't come down here. I'm covered with dirt and weeds." He cleared his throat. "Story first. I was born on the wrong side of town in a little place in Creek County... called Oilton, Oklahoma. Ever heard of it?"

Lisa nodded. "Yeah, it's about eight miles north of Drumright, I think. I went to the Drumright Technical School once for a teacher thing."

"Yeah. Okay. You want me to go on?"

"Please do. I'm fascinated, Zac. You were born on the wrong side of town. Tell me more. Is your family still in Oilton?"

"Well, I don't know who my daddy was. Some Creek Indian guy my mama said. I think that makes me a Native American bastard, doesn't it? Maybe Creek. Who knows?"

Chapter Nine

"Is your mom still in Oilton?" Zac's laughing words had brought a tiny frisson of sadness into her thinking. Bless his heart.

"I don't think so, Miss Lisa. My mother was always so drunk when I was little that I doubt she lasted long. Once when I was about five I couldn't find her and I searched for her all day long and all over that whole town."

"Oh, bless your little heart," Lisa murmured the words.

Zac looked down at her and grinned. "No use feeling sorry for me. I always thought if she didn't want me I didn't want her neither, so I never give her loss any thought except now, for your benefit, of course."

"I'm so sorry, Zac."

"When I couldn't find her, I remembered I'd heard of a guy there who was running the midnight tower at a plant in Sand Springs. He drove over every night. I asked if I could ride over with him that night, lied a little, said I was meeting Mom in Sand Springs and he took me with him in his old car. When we got there, I hid in someone else's truck which was parked in his company's parking lot 'cause I was sleepy and hey-hey! When I woke up, still in the back of that truck, it was the next morning and I was in Tulsa. Been here ever since. Getting by the best I could."

"Oh, Zac. That little boy. Makes me want to cry."

"Well, I'm okay. I'm here, Miss Hall. Grown up. Big. Working hard. I made it okay, didn't I?" He took her hand in both of his. She felt the calluses on his palms.

"Please call me Lisa." She looked up at him. He not only had physical strength, he must also have had strength of character, to have lived on the streets to become a hard worker rather than a thief or a drunk or a bum. She could only imagine the kind of life that the little boy had lived on the streets of a big town like Tulsa. He was not only gorgeous—he was highly intelligent to have survived to be so wonderful, to be this sweet beautiful man sitting beside her.

"Zac, you overcame so much. Thanks for confessing all that. I know you don't need my pity—but I was serious about you using my guestroom. Come on. Let's go get your stuff from the shed."

"Honey, that wasn't my confession. That was my story. Wait until you hear the confession before we make any big moves. You might never speak to me again."

Oh God. Had he killed someone? Raped a woman? Had to steal to live? What could he possibly confess that would be worse than the story he'd already told? Pity for that little motherless Zac rushed through her.

Chapter Ten

Zac picked up the envelope full of notes and tapped it on his knee.

"This is hard for me, school teacher lady. I don't never tell *anyone* this. I know how to survive and I know how to work but the thing that shames me is this..." He took a deep breath. "*I can't read or write.*"

"I've been ashamed of myself for that all these years and I learned long ago how to keep that secret from everybody but I just felt like I'd better tell you, seeing as how we seem to have feelings for each other, and you so educated and all." He looked down at the steps and went silent.

Lisa pushed the plate with the sandwich onto his knee and the iced drink toward his other side. She smiled.

"Better eat while it's still hot, Zac."

"Girl, didn't you hear me? I. Can't. Read. Not anything." He threw the envelope toward the back of the porch. "I don't know what the hell all those papers say."

"I heard you Zac and I know you've suffered over this, but this is really nothing." She leaned toward him. "Put that sandwich aside and kiss me, you lovely man."

He stood. "I just told you I can't read and you're grinning and saying it's nothing and wanting to kiss me!" His words were shouted but he put his hands on her shoulders and bent to touch his lips to her cheek.

"On my mouth, Zac." She murmured and closed her eyes then held her face up to receive a real kiss. The odor from the beer he'd had was barely noticeable.

His lips were cool from the iced drink yet they warmed as he pulled her closely against himself. The touch of his large body stunned her. He pressed his arousal into her belly and deepened the kiss. His heated tongue demanded more. Lisa felt the bones in her body melting to his touch.

He pulled slightly away and cupped her face with his strong, work roughened hands.

"Aw, I can't help wanting you girl. You're the sweetest thing I ever seen. Let's go look at that guest room, little school teacher."

Chapter Eleven

"My confession don't seem to bother you at all." Zac turned on his side and looked into Lisa's eyes. "You're the most educated woman I've ever known and the fact that I can't read don't seem to make any impression on you at all."

Lisa pulled him toward herself to tempt him to kiss her again.

"Who am I, Zac?" She whispered.

"Miss Lisa Hall, teacher, and I think I might be in love with you." She felt him hardening again. Wow. He loved her.

"Yeah. Teacher. Do you know what I do every day, Zac?"

"Uh huh." He pulled her leg over his body so she could be on top. "You teach."

Lisa grinned. "I teach people to read, Zac. *To read*! You're never going to be able to confess illiteracy again. You're so smart."

He entered her again and she tightened around him. "We're gonna start with L-O-V-E, darling."

Chapter Twelve

When Lisa awakened she put her hand into the indentation in the pillow next to her. He was gone! "Probably in the bathroom," she told herself, but when she'd searched the house and yard she realized Zac truly was gone. She dressed for school and raced to the locked side of the shed.

Gone! His bags, his mirror, his bedroll—all gone. He'd left her without a word. What had happened? Why had he gone without a word?

Lisa's gaze searched Tulsa's streets as she drove, her heart a leaden ball of misery within her. He'd gone, taken everything with him, left no explanation. Why had this happened just as they were discovering each other, just as he'd confessed all his innermost secrets?

The teacher's lounge in the little prefab seemed cold and cheerless because Marsha wasn't there. When the other teachers asked about Zac she told them he'd moved on and she didn't know if he'd get to their yards or not.

She slumped in her chair, praying that Mr. Kelly wouldn't show up to add to her despair. Where did one go to search for a homeless person in this town? Salvation Army? John 3:16 Mission? The Day Center on Brady? Maybe she'd go to the police.

The police? No, not the police. Might get Zac into trouble doing that.

But she could search on her own. Where did homeless people gather if they weren't in the places particularly established for their benefit?

Marsha or Cotton would know. She'd write down the possible places where homeless men gathered and she'd look in every one of them for her Zac. If he didn't want her for some reason, he'd have to tell her to her face.

She still couldn't believe they'd gotten so close, even gone to bed together and *then* he'd disappeared.

Was it because he'd told her his secrets?

The first graders seemed to sense her depression and they worked hard to try to please her. Maybe Zac would be at the house when she went home.

At the end of the day Lisa slipped into Marsha's prefab to ask about places where homeless people congregated. Marsha called Cotton for that information.

Her friends were trying to help her so she felt a bit better. She'd search every area Zac might have fled to. She *knew* why he'd gone.

He'd thought she was too good for him. He'd already indicated that with his "Miss Halls" and his, "Don't sit by me, I stink," and all the other things he'd done to distance himself from her, even though they were almost irresistibly drawn to each other.

She shivered when she relived their time in her bed the night before. Zac had been wonderful and he'd made her feel wonderful as well. She couldn't let such a magnificent meeting of hearts and bodies disappear from her life just because of a man's stupid feeling of inferiority.

She'd look for Zac and she'd find him.

"Cotton says they are a couple of places he might be. The area on the railroad tracks west of downtown or under the bridge on 41st street or maybe that empty building downtown.

"Let me write this down, Marsha. Tell Cotton thanks. He may have saved my life."

Marsha's only retort was a huffed out, "I told you that you were a gonner, girl."

She drove to the Under the Bridge area and climbed down to talk to the occupants with no luck. One of the men in the lair said he'd seen Zac earlier but didn't know where he'd gone.

This pleased Lisa and frightened her as well. The man's knowledge of Zac proved the truth of his story of growing up on Tulsa's streets. For him to be quite well-known amongst the homeless population *under a bridge* was a bit frightening to Lisa. She drove on to the dike area close to Sand Springs.

Over the dike proved to be somewhat like a small city of tents, shacks and squared off bed roll areas. "Now," one of the older women told her, "He ain't got no place over here. We're pretty full-up as it is, hon. But if I see him I'll tell him a pretty girl was a looking for him. He like pretty girls I think. What's your name, hon?"

"I'm his teacher," Lisa felt a spurt of jealousy hearing that Zac liked "pretty girls," but she quelled the feeling. *He'd be an unusual young man if he didn't like pretty girls,* Lisa thought. She thanked the woman and headed for the supposedly vacant building downtown.

Two pretty and very young women were handing out food packets, sacks containing peanuts or chips to the people pouring into the alley. Most of the folks had already started on their food as Lisa parked and slipped into the crowd. When the one called Deborah started a line for small bags of fruit, Lisa broke into the line.

"Sorry Deborah, I don't want a tangerine. I'm looking for Zac Freeman. Do you know him?"

"Oh, yeah. I haven't seen Zac today. Brandy-Lea," she called to the other girl. "Has Zac been here? Have you seen him?"

Lisa's heart sank when Brandy-Lea shook her head no and looked blank. Where the hell was the man? *Her* man. Hiding from their love was unacceptable behavior.

"Deb, you and Brandy-Lea keep an eye out for him. If you see him, tell him his school teacher is looking for him."

"His school teacher?"

"Yeah. My name is Lisa Hall." She waved thanks to the two staring youngsters and raced to her car.

"Better go home," she told herself, "He might be back there by now."

At home she cried helplessly and fell into her bed.

Chapter Thirteen

When a sound in the yard alerted her, Lisa walked into her kitchen, grabbed a two foot carved wooden spoon from the wall and stepped into the area where she would be behind the wooden kitchen door if it opened.

She clenched her teeth, raised the huge wooden spoon, ready to strike. Jerk! Anger roiled through her entire body.

She let Zac move into the kitchen then she brought her wooden weapon down hard across his backside.

"What the f...?" He whirled, fists lifted.

She hit him again.

"Where the hell have you been?"

Chapter Fourteen

His laughter infuriated her even further. She lifted the spoon once again. Zac pulled her close, imprisoning her against his hard body.

"Wow, Teach. You're a little wildcat." He kissed the angry O of her mouth. "Do you beat them first graders?"

Lisa had to laugh at that. "I would if they walked out of class without telling me where they were going or when they'd be back."

He kissed her again.

"I hear you been looking for me, Lisa. Looks like the whole town has been alerted to the fact that a school teacher is looking for Zac Freeman."

"You think that's funny, do you?"

"No babe. You hitting me with a spoon is kinda funny, but I'm here! Guess I'm thrilled that my little Teach would go to all the dirty nooks and crannies in Tulsa looking for me. Me! One of them homeless guys."

Tears rose in her eyes. "Have you left me? Do you really want to leave what we have?" She lifted the edge of his tee shirt to wipe her eyes. "I don't want you to think I'm trying to force you to stay here."

"I'm a dumb guy who cleans yards, Lisa. Awful hard for me to believe a bastard like me would be important to a woman like you with all your degrees."

"Oh, Zac...," she began.

He interrupted her. "But you do want me. Your journeys around all them rat holes in town, has convinced me. I'm back to stay. I guess... if you still want me."

Lisa broke into serious sobs when he lifted the wooden spoon to its hook on the wall.

"I do want you, you bad boy. Don't ever do that to me again."

He lifted Lisa into his arms and kissed her as he carried her. They made the kiss last across the dining room through the hall and into her bedroom.

Chapter Fifteen

Later, when they'd dressed and gone outside for the cooler air, Lisa pointed at the dusty area to the right of the back steps. "That will be our board, Zac."

"Our board?"

"Our chalkboard. And if you'll go find a long stick, that'll be our chalk."

"Chalk?"

"Yep. You're going to learn to read, Zac, and smart as you are, the process isn't going to take long."

Zac sprinted down the steps and headed for the cluster of trees near the alley, tore off a limb and raced back to Lisa. He presented the stick to her with a flourish.

"Your chalk, Teach."

"*Your* chalk, darling boy," she wrapped her hand around his and led him to trace a large L in the dust below.

"This is an 'L,' Zac. The first letter in the word love." She wrote L-O-V-E, saying each letter as she wrote. "Now write an 'L' by yourself."

Zac gripped the stick and drew a huge 'L.' He grinned as he drew, then added O-V-E.

"What word is that?"

"Love." He pulled her close and whispered. "I did learn to spell the naughty 'F' word for love when I was a kid. I even wrote it on some walls." He dropped the stick and embraced her. "I can read two words for what we feel, Lisa, and both words are important."

"Write both words in the air, *then* let's go back inside."

"Write in the air?"

"Yeah." Lisa traced an 'L' in the air in front of them. "Let the air be your chalkboard and let your finger be the chalk."

Both traced L-O-V-E and F-U-C-K in the air.

"Let's go back to bed." Lisa could see that the writing in the air had caused Zac to once again harden with desire.

Chapter Sixteen

Lisa knew her first graders loved singing the Alphabet song. She helped them finish up "The Alphabet Song" with the words, "Now I've said my ABC's, tell me what you think of me!" Lisa wasn't surprised to hear Kelly's voice from the open door.

"I'll tell you what I think of you, Miss Hall. I think you do way too much singing and dancing and playing with these here kids. They need to be working, not laughing and dancing and singing all the time."

She stared at the man who stood in the classroom doorway.

"You old bastard." The words slipped out before she could control herself. She remembered Marsha cautioning her about being snippy with the principal.

"Just remember Lisa, everyone has to deal with a boss. You can't backtalk that old boy Kelly, without some repercussions. We just have to learn to live with his speech and behavior if we want to keep working."

Lisa pressed her lips tightly together. She knew Marsha was right, but being "self-employed" was looking better and better. Anyway, she couldn't call back her words.

"What did you say?" Kelly repeated his question.

"I said, 'You old bastard,' and I shouldn't have said it. Or maybe that's giving the word *bastard* a bad name. I'm gone right now, Mr. Kelly. A little sick time. You can take over my class for the rest of the day." Lisa turned to her first graders. "Kids, I have to go but Mr. Kelley is going to work with you for the last hour this afternoon. Have a good time. Work hard for Mr. Kelly. I love all of you. See you on Monday." Lisa walked briskly from the prefab, headed toward the teacher parking lot.

Chapter Seventeen

"I think I almost quit my job, Zac. I smart mouthed my boss. I'll probably go back to finish the semester, but that's all, I've decided."

"My God. Why?"

"Old Lester insulted me."

"Insulted you? Where is he now? I'll beat the shit out of that creep."

"No, we're through with him. Think of it this way. I'm going to be your new partner. I wanted to be here with you, big guy."

"I don't have anything to offer you, Teach."

"You're only the best looking, hardest working man I've ever met. We may be going into business together, Zac."

"Business? I done told you, girl, I still don't know how to read and write. How can I run a business?"

Lisa cradled Zac's face in both of her hands. She had to be careful about this but she knew she could persuade the lovely Zac if she could find the right words.

"Not even the yard and garden business? I can do any reading and writing we'll need, big boy, but I don't know a blessed thing about gardening, so I guess we can't start a company in that case, can we?"

Zac grinned and turned his face to kiss the palm of her left hand, his dimple flashing.

Un huh. She felt a rush of gratitude that God or Fate or Providence or whatever had put her into a position to meet this man, this lovely, interesting man.

"I'll make a deal with you, little one. Soon as I can read a copy of a newspaper I'll go have cards made, then we'll be business partners. Guess we'll need to come up with a company name someday. How about this? When I can read a newspaper we can get married. That's so you won't be ashamed to introduce me as your husband."

"I'd never be ashamed to introduce you, Zac. Anyway, reading a newspaper should be possible for you within the month, darling boy. You can practice the alphabet and try reading new words when you're working."

"You ain't going to help me?"

"Oh, I will when I'm here, but I'm still under contract. I'll have to go back to school every day until the first of June. You can do a lot to prepare yourself for reading by learning the alphabet. Do you like to sing?"

"Alphabet? That's all the letters?"

"Yeah, the ABC's. The ABC's are also called the alphabet. Let's start right now. I'll sing the Alphabet song first and you listen, then we'll sing together, okay?"

Zac's "okay" sounded dubious, Lisa mused. *He thinks he can't do this, but if I can teach twenty five six or seven year-olds to do it in an hour, Zac can be singing the alphabet in minutes. Drawing the letters will require a bit more work from both of us.*

Lisa took a deep breath.

"A B C D E F G,
H I J K, L M N O P,
Q R S T U and V,
W, X and Y and Z.
Now I've said my ABC's,
tell me what you think of me."

Her voice rang out across her manicured yard.
"Sing it one more time, Miss Lisa."
"Okay. Singing is a great way to learn almost anything. I discovered that when I first began teaching."
In minutes Lisa's backsteps and the huge lot echoed around them with "The Alphabet Song" as a duet. They sang the ditty over and over again.
"That deep voice of yours sure sounds good under my soprano. Wonder what the neighbors think?" A giggle escaped Lisa's lips.
"They might think we're having school over here." Zac picked up the stick and looked over the porch rail. "Now comes the hard part, I guess."
Lisa guided his hand to write a big Z.
"The last letter in the alphabet is the first letter in your first name, Zac. Let's write your name." She directed his hand to a big ZAC in the dust below. He then wrote his name in the air. "Did you already know how to write your name?"
"Not exactly. But I've always knowed that the zigzag letter was how my name started. I always liked the look of that letter when I had to sign something I just wrote the Z and a little line after it, then the big F and a little line after it. Kinda like lightning, ain't it?"
"You've certainly been like lightning in my life, Zac. Bright, unexpected, sent to me by God, perhaps."

Chapter Eighteen

In November, Lisa bought frozen turkey with the idea of baking it for Zac and herself. Should she have Marsha and her Cotton Linsley over also? She'd discuss it with Zac. The big read would take place at the Thanksgiving table she decided. She'd have the newspaper ready. If he could read the newspaper she'd consider it a proposal.

In the teacher's lounge she approached Marsha with a Thanksgiving dinner invitation, then asked for any special hints about cooking a turkey.

"You mean *this* is the first time you've ever baked a turkey?"

"I'm getting ready to be a wife so, *yes*, this is my first turkey bake experience. I want it to be good."

"Cotton and I will be there. I'll email you the recipe for your bird. You and this guy must be pretty serious, I guess… you already talking about being a wife."

Chapter Nineteen

Reading and writing words in the dirt and in the air became a pleasant evening pastime for Zac and Lisa. "Scholar" became her pet nickname for the man who had mowed his way into her life. Teaching first graders and trying to bear her principal's remarks took a good portion of each day, but evenings and weekends were their own.

"Let's all tell what we're thankful for." Lisa carried her late mother's 'Turkey Platter' into the dining room. Zac jumped up to take the heavy baked bird. He put the platter on the round table at the side where Lisa had been sitting.

"Put the bird in front of you, Zac. You can do the carving for us. I'll get my sharp knife." When she returned with the knife she also carried the long wooden spoon and placed it in the center of the table.

"Marsha, remember this lovely ornamental spoon that you brought me from your trip to Jamaica?"

Marsha smiled and nodded. "I bought one for myself, also, kiddo. They're hand carved and I thought them to be so interesting looking."

Zac nudged Cotton. "They can be pretty dangerous, as well. You ever had a big wooden spoon laid over your backside by an angry woman?"

Cotton grinned. "Nope. I try to keep on Marsha's good side. Don't want a school teacher whipping me, not at my age."

"I've learned my lesson, too, friend. Always ask permission to leave the room."

Cotton laughed and nodded. "Right on."

When they were all seated and ready to tell what they were thankful for, Lisa pulled out an old copy of the newspaper, *USA Today*, opened the paper and pointed to a paragraph at random.

"Read this for us Zac, before we give thanks."

Zac glanced at the paragraph. "You a golfer, Lisa?" Then he smiled and read aloud:

> Mickelson made bogeys on the final two holes to fall to a 70, taking three putts in the 17th and hitting his tee shot into the trees on the 18th.

"Hey Zac, reading from that newspaper will be your downfall, boy," Marsha grinned at Cotton. "She expects the man to marry her now. She told me so at school."

"I'm willing!" Zac's words rang out. "Meeting up with this lady is the one thing I am most thankful for, folks... and I don't mind admitting that."

"I accept your lovely proposal in front of witnesses, Zachary." She smiled at his look of surprise. "Yeah, Zachary is the long word that 'Zac' stands for, hon. So our marriage would make me Mrs. Zachary Freeman, a very lucky woman."

In December, Marsha and Cotton, a newly ordained Baptist preacher and 26 excited first graders attended the wedding of Lisa Hall and Zachary Freeman in a portable classroom at Tulsa elementary school and all present toasted the affair with cans of cold Dr. Pepper held high.

Mr. Kelly was not invited to the ceremony.

LaVergne, TN USA
12 August 2010
193078LV00002B/3/P